THE TWO OF US

I liked Charles. I liked him as a friend, but I didn't want people to think we were going out together, that we were a couple. If that happened, I wouldn't get a chance for a real boyfriend at all.

It hardly seemed fair. Nothing that had happened since I arrived at Grandma's seemed fair—the accidents with Melissa and O.P., the tryouts for the play, and now Charles. It all seemed like some huge plot to make sure I never achieved my dream.

If only I could start this whole thing over, I thought longingly. *If only I could just pretend the last two weeks had never happened and just walk in again as a new person.*

Suddenly an idea came to me.

D0563209

Bantam Sweet Dreams Romances
Ask your bookseller for the books you have missed

#1 P.S. I LOVE YOU
#2 THE POPULARITY PLAN
#3 LAURIE'S SONG
#4 PRINCESS AMY
#5 LITTLE SISTER
#6 CALIFORNIA GIRL
#7 GREEN EYES
#8 THE THOROUGHBRED
#9 COVER GIRL
#10 LOVE MATCH
#11 THE PROBLEM WITH LOVE
#12 NIGHT OF THE PROM
#13 THE SUMMER JENNY FELL
     IN LOVE
#14 DANCE OF LOVE
#15 THINKING OF YOU
#16 HOW DO YOU SAY GOODBYE
#17 ASK ANNIE
#18 TEN-BOY SUMMER
#19 LOVE SONG
#20 THE POPULARITY SUMMER
#21 ALL'S FAIR IN LOVE
#22 SECRET IDENTITY
#23 FALLING IN LOVE AGAIN
#24 THE TROUBLE WITH
     CHARLIE
#25 HER SECRET SELF
#26 IT MUST BE MAGIC
#27 TOO YOUNG FOR LOVE
#28 TRUSTING HEARTS
#29 NEVER LOVE A COWBOY
#30 LITTLE WHITE LIES
#31 TOO CLOSE FOR COMFORT
#32 DAYDREAMER
#33 DEAR AMANDA

#34 COUNTRY GIRL
#35 FORBIDDEN LOVE
#36 SUMMER DREAMS
#37 PORTRAIT OF LOVE
#38 RUNNING MATES
#39 FIRST LOVE
#40 SECRETS
#41 THE TRUTH ABOUT ME &
     BOBBY V.
#42 THE PERFECT MATCH
#43 TENDER LOVING CARE
#44 LONG DISTANCE LOVE
#45 DREAM PROM
#46 ON THIN ICE
#47 TE AMO MEANS I LOVE YOU
#48 DIAL L FOR LOVE
#49 TOO MUCH TO LOSE
#50 LIGHTS, CAMERA, LOVE
#51 MAGIC MOMENTS
#52 LOVE NOTES
#53 GHOST OF A CHANCE
#54 I CAN'T FORGET YOU
#55 SPOTLIGHT ON LOVE
#56 CAMPFIRE NIGHTS
#57 ON HER OWN
#58 RHYTHM OF LOVE
#59 PLEASE SAY YES
#60 SUMMER BREEZES
#61 EXCHANGE OF HEARTS
#62 JUST LIKE THE MOVIES
#63 KISS ME, CREEP
#64 LOVE IN THE FAST LANE
#65 THE TWO OF US
#66 LOVE TIMES TWO

The Two Of Us

Janet Quin-Harkin

BANTAM BOOKS

TORONTO • NEW YORK • LONDON • SYDNEY • AUCKLAND

RL 6, IL age 11 and up

THE TWO OF US
A Bantam Book / July 1984

*Sweet Dreams and its associated logo are registered trade-
marks of Bantam Books, Inc. Registered in U.S. Patent and
Trademark Office and elsewhere.*

Cover photo by Pat Hill

All rights reserved.
Copyright © 1984 by Janet Quin-Harkin and
Cloverdale Press Inc.
*This book may not be reproduced in whole or in part, by
mimeograph or any other means, without permission.
For information address: Bantam Books, Inc.*

ISBN 0-553-24152-2

Published simultaneously in the United States and Canada

*Bantam Books are published by Bantam Books, Inc. Its
trademark, consisting of the words "Bantam Books" and
the portrayal of a rooster, is Registered in U.S. Patent and
Trademark Office and in other countries. Marca Registrada.
Bantam Books, Inc., 666 Fifth Avenue, New York, New
York 10103.*

PRINTED IN THE UNITED STATES OF AMERICA

O   0 9 8 7 6 5 4 3 2

The
Two Of Us

Chapter One

"In my opinion there have been only two things standing between success and me," I said to Carly.

Carly was sitting on her bed in her Manhattan apartment, which was one floor below mine, eating oranges. She was playing her records as usual.

"What?" she yelled over the din.

"Could you please turn down the music a bit?" I yelled back across the room. With a look of utter amazement on her face, she rolled over, reached out a hand, and lowered the volume on the stereo. "You want me to turn down the Police?" she asked. "What are you, some kind of weirdo or something?"

"Carly, I need to talk," I said.

"OK. So talk."

"As I was attempting to say—I have been doing some serious thinking, and I've decided there

1

are only two things standing between success and me," I said.

"Your mom and your dad?" she asked.

"Make that four things then," I agreed. "I hadn't thought about them, but you're right. No, the two things I was thinking about were going to an all-girls school—"

"Definitely a stumbling block to ever finding a boyfriend," she agreed. "And what else?"

"And my big mouth," I added.

Carly grinned and spat an orange seed into the wastebasket.

"Well, it's true," I went on. "I'm always saying what comes into my head before I stop and think about it. You make enemies that way."

Carly nodded, her mouth full of orange. "But you've always had a big mouth. Remember what you called that girl in your kindergarten?"

"You mean the one who weighed five hundred pounds and always drooled?"

"That's the one. I also remember that she helped your big mouth get a little smaller by slugging out a few of your teeth," Carly said. "But why the sudden self-analysis?" she continued. "Are you making New Year's resolutions in advance? It's only October, you know."

I sat in Carly's white wicker chair and gazed out the window, watching the lights come up across the East River in Queens. I'd better add that Carly's apartment is only on the ninth floor and that I could see only a very small square of the East River and Queens between the buildings. I add this just in case you thought Carly and I were the sort of girls who lived in Manhattan penthouses. Outside, New York had a real late-October look—gray with a sky heavy with rain. I started to imagine a desert where it would be one hundred and twenty degrees in the shade and rain only once every five years.

"Earth to Stephanie," Carly called. "You didn't answer my question, and you're gazing out of the window all dreamy. Have you flipped, or are you in love?"

"I wish," I said. "I mean I wish I was in love." I turned back to Carly, who was now lying on her bed. In her tight miniskirt and pointy-toed high heels, her face half hidden behind a curtain of black hair, she looked like the sort of person I could have been if only my parents would have let me. "Look," I said. "I've got a lot on my mind, that's all. I've just found out something rather startling. If you promise not to tell another soul—"

"Oh, goody, I love secrets," Carly said, sitting upright and leaning toward me. "Is it a really good one?" She slowly tossed back her hair— she was practicing to be a model someday.

"It's my parents," I said, lowering my voice in case one of her brothers was passing the door. They've been known to threaten blackmail with my secrets before. "I got up to raid the refrigerator last night, and I overheard them talking—"

"They're getting a divorce?" Her big, mascaraed eyes got bigger.

"No such luck," I said with a grin. "My dad's company wants to send him back to Saudi Arabia for six months."

"Wow—that's great!"

3

"Shh. It's a secret, remember. But they can't decide whether to go or not."

"I'd go like a shot—think of all those rich sheiks and cute camels."

"I gather the problem is me," I said. "Mom wants to go with Dad, but she doesn't think it's a suitable place for me."

"So—you could stay on in your apartment, live on TV dinners, and bring your laundry down to my mom."

I laughed out loud at that one. "Can you see my parents—of all the parents in the whole universe—letting me stay alone anywhere?"

"So, what are they going to do with you?"

"Well, Dad wants to send me to my grandmother, his mother, because she's just moved to Connecticut and there's a good school near her."

"But?"

"But—my mother and my grandmother don't quite agree on things. My mother thinks my grandmother wouldn't be strict enough with me."

"So now you just have to wait until they decide to tell you officially," Carly said. She finished her orange and wiped her mouth with a tissue, which she then dropped into the wastebasket. "But you like your grandmother, don't you? Wouldn't you like to stay with her?"

I stared out of the window again. It had started to rain, big, fat blobs of water, chasing one another down the glass and blurring that square of the East River.

"I guess so," I said. "You've met Grandma

Beth. She's a lot of fun—not at all like my parents. And it would certainly be nice to go somewhere where nobody knows me and start over—at a real high school with boys! How about that! I might be able to turn into a normal teenager."

"Miracles don't happen that often," Carly said. "Maybe almost normal."

"Shut up and listen," I said. "I'm trying to tell you my life plan, and you keep making wise-cracks."

"OK, I'm listening," she said. "One hundred percent concentration. Go on, tell me about how you propose to turn into a normal teenager."

"Well, without Mom and Dad breathing down my neck and nobody around who remembers my bumbling big mouth, I might be able to turn into the sort of person I want to be."

"And who, pray, is that?" Carly asked, raising one eyebrow, which is a very annoying habit that she does often since she and Mr. Spock are the only ones who can do it.

"Oh, you know—pretty, popular, great boy-friend, talented singer—"

Carly laughed. "You don't need a grandmother for all that, you need a fairy godmother."

I frowned at her. "It should be possible," I said. "I don't know what you're laughing about. I know I can sing, but Mom and Dad never let me sing in public. I know I could be pretty and sexy, too, if I didn't have to wear this old uniform, and I know I could get a boyfriend if I was around boys all day, and I could be popular, too, if they didn't know me as the girl with the big mouth."

"So, go for it," Carly said. "But knowing your parents, I shouldn't be at all surprised if they didn't put you in a convent for six months—you know, the old-fashioned sort with a twelve-foot wall, where they have prayers at three in the morning and make you wear horsehair robes—"

"Most likely they'll decide not to go because of me, then run around complaining about the wonderful chance they turned down for me. Or, maybe they'll take me with them and then never let me out in case I talk to a sheik." I sank deeper into Carly's white wicker chair and gave a long sigh. "You know, as much as I love my parents, it *is* tough to be an only child."

"You can have my family anytime you want it," Carly said. "Try lining up for the bathroom a few times, and see how tough it is being an only child."

"I'd willingly line up for the bathroom if my parents would stop acting like secret service agents. Honestly, Carly, they follow me around, watch me every time I breathe, tell me what friends I can have and what clothes I can wear. Believe me, a bathroom line is a small price to pay for freedom!"

"As usual you're exaggerating," Carly said and then softened her voice, saying "You know, I'll miss you if you're away for six months."

"I'll miss you, too."

"No, you won't. You'll be too busy chasing boys, looking sexy, and singing. I'll be left behind with no upstairs neighbor. Your parents will probably rent your apartment to a horrible family with lots of little kids with runny noses who scream all night long, and all I'll do is baby-sit."

"They might rent it to a real great guy who asks you to help him with his homework—in which case you won't want me back again."

"Not me," she said. "I'm not interested. I'm staying faithful to Rick Springfield." She got up and went over to kiss his picture—or rather one of his pictures. There were pictures of him all over her walls, along with pictures of the Police, Styx, and many other rock stars and groups I couldn't identify. Carly was deeply into music. I'd like to have been, but it was hard to get deep into anything my parents wouldn't allow in the house. My parents had this theory that any music after the Beatles, and early Beatles at that, was evil and corrupting to young minds. So I had to keep my tiny transistor radio under the bedcovers at night. It was very hard for a future rock singer to be so starved for good music, and if Carly hadn't lived downstairs with the largest record collection in New York City, I'd never have survived. I went down there, also, to practice my guitar, which I'd bought from my lunch money.

"I've just thought of something," I said, mostly to interrupt the revolting spectacle of Carly slobbering all over Rick Springfield. "If I go to Grandma's house, she won't care what sort of music I play."

"Well, I hope for your sake that your parents

hurry up and make up their minds, or you'll go bananas," Carly said. "And what's more, I will, too, if you don't let me turn up my music."

She walked over to the stereo and turned it up to ear-shattering volume again.

Chapter Two

It was not easy pretending that I had no idea what my parents were plotting behind my back. I longed to come right out and say, "Hey, what's all this?" and force the truth out of them. But my parents were not like that. They liked to make decisions slowly and methodically and tell me the outcome only when they had made up their minds and were sure that the decision was good and right. They believed that children did not develop minds of their own until they reached the age of twenty-one, and until then they were to be treated like prize cats, kept well-fed and warm. Any attempt to change my parents would have blown their minds—don't think I hadn't tried!

So, for about a week I went around with an innocent look on my face—which wasn't easy. In fact, Carly almost blew the whole thing one day when she was over for dinner and made a dumb joke about camels.

"Why don't your mom and dad come out and tell you about it?" she snapped. "The suspense is killing me. What I don't understand is why they don't include you in their discussions—after all, it's your life they're screwing up, isn't it?"

I shrugged my shoulders. "They never have," I said. "It comes from having old parents. They didn't have me until they had already been married for six years. I guess they just got used to being a couple without me. They've never thought to discuss things with me, and if I try to force them, they just smile and say they're doing everything for my own good. Haven't you heard them? My dad says, 'She's not looking well. What do you think, Catherine?' And my mom answers, 'I've noticed she's been quite pale lately,' and neither of them thinks to ask me how I feel. Even if I told them I felt fine, they wouldn't believe me. Their minds would be made up that I was sick."

Carly laughed. "I only hope you don't go bananas with all that freedom at your grandma's house—that is, if you get to go there and not to the convent."

We had had that conversation a week before, and still my parents hadn't said anything to me. My mother had even bought a book of Arabic phrases and walked around muttering strange things in her throat when she thought I wasn't listening. I began to wonder if I would wake one morning and find they'd left without me. Then, finally, one evening I heard Dad on the phone to Grandma Beth, and after he had hung up, he called me into the living room.

"Stephanie, honey, we've got some big news," my mother said.

The hardest thing for me to do was not to laugh. Of course I knew exactly what they were going to say, and my mouth kept twitching at the edges while I tried to act surprised and bewildered.

"So how come you're not taking me?" I asked after they told me their plan. I thought I sounded very convincing as the hurt child. They looked, I thought, suitably guilty.

"But, Stephie—you wouldn't enjoy it one bit," my mother said. "The terrible heat—so boring. In fact, Dad's company advises against taking children, and most foreign workers have their children in boarding schools."

"You're not putting me in a boarding school!" I blurted out, feeling rather pleased with the way I was playing my part. I'd always known I was a good actress.

"Of course we're not," my father said soothingly. "Grandma Beth has offered to take you."

"You'd like to stay with Grandma Beth, wouldn't you, honey?" my mother asked.

"I guess so," I said, carrying on my great act and resisting the temptation to jump up and down and shout, "Whoopee!" Instead I said, "But I'll miss you both."

That time the acting was almost too good, and I was afraid I had blown it when my mother wailed, "Oh, Frank, I do hope we're doing the right thing. Perhaps it would be best if I stayed with her after all."

The next two weeks I tried to assure her that

11

I would survive with Grandma. I also tried to hide my growing excitement about my six months of freedom. The ride up to Connecticut on that Saturday seemed endless. My mother continued to worry out loud, and several times I was afraid they would turn the car around and take me back home. She worried about everything from whether I would remember to wear a hat on cold days to whether Grandma Beth would be careful enough to check the kids I hung out with. The way she went on, you'd have thought I'd be involved with the Hell's Angels within a week—and, no doubt, suffering from an ear infection because I'd ridden on one of their motorcycles without a hat!

I had asked to travel alone to Grandma's house. It was a perfectly easy trip by train, and any other sixteen-year-old could have made it with no problem. But they would just as soon have let me travel to Antarctica alone. So I sat in the backseat of our car, looking out of the window and trying to shut out my mother's last-minute instructions while the rich Connecticut countryside flashed past us. A few of the trees were still dressed in late fall colors, framing white houses with the last of the oranges, yellows, and browns. I had never lived in the country before, and it dawned on me that living in a small town would be an experience in itself, especially after New York. Imagine! In a small town you could get to know everybody, and you could walk to friends' houses in the evenings. The more I thought about it the better it sounded.

I shut my eyes and started to make plans. How would I dress? I'd need more new clothes after all my years in a green-checked uniform. And how would I make friends? Maybe there was a cute boy living down the block from Grandma, and maybe I'd try out for chorus and they'd immediately ask me to sing a solo. There were all sorts of exciting maybes, and although my heart was beating nervously, it was a good, hopeful sort of nervousness.

As we drove through Hartford, my parents stepped up their panic campaign.

"Oh, Frank, what will we do if she gets sick and we're so far away? Maybe this wasn't such a good idea. . . ."

At the same time my father droned out a constant lecture: "Now remember, Stephanie, no late nights, and do your homework. And remember that you will be coming into close contact with boys; just remember the kind of friends we like you to make."

He said it in the tone of voice that you would use to say, "Now remember, you will be coming into contact with cannibals or twelve-foot hairy monsters." I sighed and said, "Yes, Dad, no, Dad," at intervals, which actually kept him happy.

In the end Mom's constant worrying started me off, too. What if I didn't make any friends for the whole six months—what if nobody even spoke to me and what if it was the sort of snobby school where they didn't like outsiders? How was I going to survive without Carly for six months?

"Call me," she had said when I left. "And tell me how horribly sexy, popular, and famous you've become." Then she had given me an Adam Ant record just like hers. "Just think, you'll actually be able to play this for once," she said.

I thought about that then, and it cheered me up again. At Grandma's house I could do what I wanted to do. No more parents bearing down on me.

We drove down the main street of Grandma's little town. We passed a wooden church which was set back among large, old maple trees; it looked right out of Paul Revere's times. A pale late-afternoon sun filtered through the tree branches, and children were playing in a small, well-kept park. It was all very sleepy and peaceful, and for someone born and brought up in New York City, as foreign as Timbuktu.

We turned off the main street onto a wide, tree-lined avenue. Most of the maples were bare, and leaves were lying thick on the sidewalks. Neatly raked piles stood in the yards of most of the houses. Dad stopped the car in front of a large, rolling lawn with a small, white wooden cottage set far back from the street.

My grandmother had moved away from New York City four months before, and this was the first time we had visited her in her new Connecticut home.

"Well, who would have thought your mother would end up in a place like this?" my mother asked.

"What's wrong with it?" my father asked, springing to the defense of his mother.

"Nothing's wrong with it," my mother said. "It's just not like your mother, that's all. It's so folksy, and she was always so modern."

"Well, I like it," I said firmly. It was a friendly looking house, and I felt right away that it liked me, too. Its windows seemed to wink encouragement in the late-afternoon sun.

"We can get her luggage in a minute, Frank," my mother said to my father, who was about to open the trunk. "For heaven's sake, let's go inside and say hello first." She led the way up a brick path and three brick steps to a wooden porch and a dark green front door. We rang the bell.

"Come on in, it's open," called a voice. We pushed the door and went inside. It was funny to see Grandma's furniture in this new setting. Somehow it looked even more elegant, and her Oriental rugs looked better against the polished hardwood floors.

"Where are you, Mom? It's us," Dad called.

"Through here, Frank," came Grandmother's voice, sounding tired, faint, and far off.

We looked at one another in alarm as we hurried through the house to a big family room at the back. Grandma was lying back in an armchair, her eyes closed. She opened them as we came in.

"Forgive me for not getting up," she said weakly. "But just right now I don't feel up to it."

"What's wrong, Mother, are you sick?" my father asked, hurrying over to kneel beside her.

A tired smile crossed her face. "No, Frank, I'm not sick. I have just got to face the fact that

15

I can no longer run more than five miles. That last mile just finished me off in the six-point-two-mile race today—especially since it was all uphill. I'd have won the medal for the over-fifties if it hadn't been for that wretched hill."

"Mother," my father said, as if he were talking to a naughty child, "you've got to start acting sensibly."

"Who says so?" Grandma asked, sitting upright and no longer looking tired. "When I start acting sensibly, they can come and nail me in my coffin!"

Chapter Three

You may be wondering about my grandmother. She is not exactly your classic grandmother type who bakes cookies and does crochet in a rocking chair. As long as I've known her, she's been a physical fitness nut. How she managed to produce anyone as flabby and unathletic as my father, I do not know! When she isn't jogging, she's playing tennis or swimming. She looks terrific, has a slim figure and neat, blondish-gray hair. In fact, she looks more like the president of a bank or something than somebody's grandmother. What's more, she has more energy than I do.

My parents think she's quite crazy and can't understand why she won't start acting her age. They want her to realize that anybody over seventy ought to be sitting in a rocking chair making afghans. Grandma just laughs at them and says that when she decides to be old, she will let them know.

So you can imagine I was looking forward to staying with Grandma Beth. When she lived in New York, we saw quite a lot of her, though only for short visits because she made my father nervous and my mother mad. Those visits were a glimpse of freedom for me. Everything forbidden at home was allowed at Grandma's. And now I would have more than a glimpse. I would have six whole months in which I could do just what I wanted for the first time in my life.

But Grandma Beth had her own ideas about how to bring up a teenager. We had just finished the tearful goodbye scene, in which the only person who hadn't cried was Grandma. I have to confess that I cried a little—my parents may not have been the most ideal, but they were the only ones I had, and they were going halfway around the world. They might be kidnapped by Bedouins or trampled by camels or even buried in a desert sandstorm.

I watched our familiar gray Honda drive away and was just wiping the tears from my cheeks when Grandma started chattering.

"We're going to have a grand time together, Stephanie. It's been such a long while since I've spent time with you. You can come jogging with me, and my friend Louise has a son your age whom I'd love you to meet."

As she was going on in her excited manner, she was turning me around and inspecting me at arm's length as though I were a store dummy. "Hmmm," she continued, "I have only six months to undo some of the harm that your parents

18

have done over the past sixteen years. But there's some hope for you yet—"

"What are you talking about—'hope'?" I interrupted. "You make it sound like my parents abused me as a child."

"Abused, maybe not," replied Grandma. "But they have managed to thoroughly overprotect you. Don't tell me you aren't glad to escape that old-fashioned school they force you to go to! A school full of pampered girls is what it is. I bet the biggest problem that each of them has ever faced is who is going to win the art contest! You have been totally sheltered. I bet you don't even know how to talk to a boy."

"I'll meet boys in college. And my friend Carly is more experienced with boys than I, and she teaches me."

"Well," said Grandma, "it's not just the school that I object to. Your parents never once let you make your own mistakes. Your mother makes all of your decisions for you—chooses your clothes, feeds you as though you were a starving child. Just look at you." And she continued her examination of me, eyeing me up and down. "You look like you run home for milk and cookies every day after school."

"Gee, thanks a lot," I said, taking her hint that I could stand to lose a few pounds. "You really know how to boost a girl's ego." I didn't bother correcting her. In fact, I never ran home from school to drink milk and eat cookies. I tried to stay away as long as possible after school and that meant hanging around the Häagen-Dazs ice-cream store and pizza parlors. Carly and I were convinced that we were going to find the best pizza in all of New York—and that meant a lot of sampling.

Grandma, on the other hand, was known for her health food and exercise programs. Carrot sticks and bean sprouts were her idea of delicious foods. And exercise! The word made me shudder. I used to brag about having invented an excuse to get out of every session of body conditioning and swimming.

"Besides," I said, trying to defend myself against Grandma's critical eye, "I weigh well within the limits set for my height and age."

"Those limits were written by fat people," Grandma shot back. "But just think, honey, if we could trim you down a bit, the boys might just find you even more irresistible than you already are." And her eyes twinkled kindly.

Grandma knew how to get me where it counted. I had never really thought about seeing boys on a daily basis before. Sure, I thought about boys all the time, but suddenly I remembered that every day that I went to school I would be seen by loads of boys. I started getting a little nervous and stopped arguing with Grandma, whose good nature was hard to resist.

By this time she had picked up my two heavy suitcases and was starting to trot up the stairs. I followed her up a wooden staircase so low I had to duck my head to keep from banging it on the ceiling. We wound through a narrow landing, where a small window threw a pool of light on a vase of dried flowers, and stepped into an attic bedroom that seemed very old. It smelled old, too—a mixture of furniture polish, dried flowers, and mothballs, but it was a good smell. It made the bedroom friendly. And the yellow-and-white gingham dustruffle curtains and pillows on the white window seat heightened the warm atmosphere.

"I'll leave you to unpack," Grandma said. "Yell if you want more hangers." Then she went.

I walked over to the window, put one knee up on the window seat, and looked out. My window overlooked the street. I peered up and down, looking for signs of life, especially for those of that cute boy whom I had imagined next door. All I saw was an old man who shuffled out to get a newspaper, then shuffled in again. Two old women walked past with two old dogs on leashes. It began to look as if the average age of the neighborhood was seventy or eighty. No motorbikes or ten-speeds left in driveways. No sounds of loud music echoing down the block.

So much for the cute boy next door, I thought as bubble number one burst. I hung up my clothes. Needless to say, I did not need any more hangers. I'd brought hardly anything with me, for the simple reason that I owned hardly anything worth wearing. When you spend most of your life in a green-checked blouse, gray skirt, and green knee socks, you don't have too many outfits that can be worn in the real world. My mother had bought me a couple of new outfits, but they were terrible. I changed out of my saying-goodbye-to-my-parents outfit, which was a jumper and turtleneck that she had bought, into my one comfortable pair of jeans and my one normal T-shirt, which had "Ozzie Osmond in Concert" on the front. My last birthday present from Carly!

There was a big mirror over the vanity, one of those triple mirrors that show you from all sides. I eyed myself critically as I changed my clothes. Was I really fat? I didn't bulge anywhere, except in the right places. In fact, I wasn't bad-looking at all. True, my hair was a sort of an in-between shade of dark brown, but it had enough curl to make it bounce. And my eyes were an interesting hazel that seemed to change with the color I was wearing. Maybe I could stand to lose a pound or two around the hips, but with the right clothes and the right makeup and the right hairstyle, surely some boy would finally notice me!

Grandma is a weird one, all right, I thought to myself. *What does she have in mind for me these six months?* And that's when it hit me. She had done a marvelous job of making me forget about my parents' leaving and about leaving my home. She had made me think about the future in my new home. Already she had me plotting, planning, and thinking about boys. I felt as if it were a new year and I was beginning again.

Chapter Four

One thing I learned very quickly about Grandma Beth was that she ate an awful lot of salads. I do not like salads. I am of the firm opinion that if we had been designed to eat salads, we would have been born with rabbit teeth. We also didn't eat much sugar, which meant no soda and no cakes for dessert. Grandma claimed she didn't even like chocolate, and I thought that was so crazy that I teased her about getting senile in her old age.

My very first morning there, which happened to be Sunday, I found out how crazy she was when she forced me into her exercise program. I'd just had my first breakfast with her, my first Sunday-morning breakfast in living memory with no bacon, no sausage, and no pancakes with blueberry syrup. Grandma just had plain yogurt and wheat toast—I mean, yuck! I chose scrambled eggs over that, but what a choice. Outside was a gray, bitterly cold day, and I was wondering what I would do with myself when I knew nobody. I didn't want to have to sit around at home worrying about the new school I would have to start the next day.

As it turned out, I didn't have to worry about sitting around. Right after breakfast Grandma appeared in her purple jogging suit and white Nikes.

"OK. Go get changed," she said like a drill sergeant. "Time for our morning jog."

"You want us to go jogging in this?" I asked, my voice squeaking as I rolled my eyes toward the gloom outside the window.

"What's wrong with it? Perfect jogging weather, in fact," she said, doing stretches on the Persian rug.

"But, Grandma—it's freezing out there, and it's Sunday. You know, day of rest and gladness and all that!"

"No ifs ands or buts, young woman," she said firmly. "It will do you the world of good, and you'll feel like a new person."

"It'll do that all right," I muttered. "A dead person, probably."

Unwillingly I changed into my warm-ups and tennis shoes. And when I went downstairs, Grandma eyed them suspiciously.

"Don't you have any proper running shoes?" she asked.

"These were all I needed for PE at school," I said. I didn't mention that they looked almost new because I had managed to avoid nine-tenths of my PE classes at school.

My grandmother sighed. "No wonder you don't

enjoy running," she said. "With horrible flat-footed things like those, nobody could enjoy running. We'll get you a proper pair tomorrow. You'll ruin your feet in those—especially with the amount of weight you're carrying!" she added with a teasing grin.

"Oh, Grandma, you don't have to spend your money on me," I said sweetly. "I really can do without a new pair of running shoes. I just won't come jogging, that's all."

"Go on with you," she said, giving me a friendly push. "You're not getting out of it that easily. I have set myself the monumental task of turning you into the sort of granddaughter I can be proud of, and I'm not a quitter."

She escorted me to the front door. "Now this will be a very gentle introduction," she said as we walked down the brick path. The cold wind felt like ice water in my face; it took my breath away.

"We'll just trot down to the park, and then there's a nice, easy mile course we can run there," she said.

Quite frankly I didn't think I could make it as far as the end of the block, let alone the park, let alone jog around a mile course once I got there.

"Where is this park?" I gasped. "Downtown Hartford?"

"It's only around the corner," she said soothingly. "Come on, keep those legs moving."

We crossed the street at the end of the block and headed for some impressive iron gates. Grandma kept up a one-sided conversation all the way. I barely had enough breath to run, let alone talk. She chattered away, "And it's a very pleasant little park. The band plays there during the summer, and I have heard that the spring flowers are really lovely. I adored jogging past the summer flowers when everything was in full bloom. It's a bit depressing now, I know, but wait for the spring. And it's not snowing, which is a thing to be grateful for."

For a moment I wished it were snowing, then we couldn't have jogged around the park, could we? On the other hand, knowing my grandmother, we would probably be like the mail service and jog through rain, snow, sleet, or hail—maybe even pushing snowplows to do it!

There was a track around the perimeter of the park, a smooth dirt surface that I was sure would have looked appealing to a runner. To me it looked like a torture chamber.

"Once around is a mile," Grandma said. "Let's see how long it takes you."

She ran ahead of me, obviously bored by my slow pace. I stumbled along behind her. It was a nice track, as tracks go. Evergreens were growing on either side of the track. Seeing them gave me an idea: I could slip between the bushes and cut across the park to the other side. No one need ever know I'd save myself half a mile. . . . Swiftly I dodged through the bushes, feeling a bit like a criminal, and sprinted across to the bushes on the other side. I was just looking for a place to wriggle through and rest before resuming my jog when a voice behind me spoke: "You cheated."

I spun around, expecting to see Grandma's teasing smile, but it wasn't Grandma at all. It was a girl of about my age with a friendly, freckled face. Her nose and cheeks were bright red from the cold wind. Her hair was hidden under a red ski cap, and she was wearing a red and white ski sweater.

I looked around to make sure she was talking to me, but there was no one else in sight.

"Did you say something?" I asked cautiously.

She grinned at me, a big, wide grin showing a mouth full of braces. "I said I just caught you cheating, that's all," she said.

"I don't know what you're talking about," I said frostily.

"Sure you do," she said, laughing. "You cut across from the other side of the track—you only ran half a mile, instead of a mile."

"And what if I did?" I said, feeling my face growing red from anger as well as the cold wind. "It really isn't any of your business—or is it a hobby of yours to go checking up on strangers?"

"Hey, hold your hair on," she said easily. "I'm not accusing you or anything—it was just funny to see you do that because my friends and I started doing the same thing when we had jogging in PE. We'd hang back until everyone was ahead of us, then cut across and sneak out of the bushes to finish with everyone else. The PE teacher never caught us, either." She broke into a high-pitched laugh. "So I guess that means we're the same sort of person," she added.

"Unathletic but sneaky?" I asked, warming up to her high spirits.

"I prefer to say smart and imaginative," she said. "I'm Laurie Wilson, by the way. Are you new in town or just visiting?"

"I'm Stephanie Fenton. I'm staying with my grandmother for six months."

"So you'll be coming to our school?"

"Is there more than one?"

"No."

"Then I'll be coming."

"That's great," she said. "Where did you go to school before?"

"New York City."

"Wow—then you'll find our little school a bit of a letdown. We only have five hundred kids and crumbling old buildings, and we don't even have a decent football team."

"That doesn't worry me," I said. "I come from a school with no football team at all."

"No football team?" She looked amazed.

"Well, you could hardly expect a hundred and fifty girls to play football, could you?"

She looked at me as if I had just told her I was from Mars. "You went to an all-girls school?" she asked.

"That's right."

"You poor thing. How did you survive with no boys all day?"

"You don't miss what you've never had, I guess." I shrugged.

We started to walk together along the track, falling into step with each other. Laurie was silent for a while then she said, "I always thought the boys around here weren't so hot—but they're sure better than nothing. We'll have to help you make up for lost time."

"Thanks, I'd appreciate that," I said. "That's exactly what I had planned to do."

"Of course, the really cute boys are unavailable," she said, "because they all hang around with Melissa Anderson and her group."

"Melissa Anderson?"

"The number-one hotshot girl," she said, wrinkling her nose. "You know the sort—Miss Popularity, track star, acting star, everything star—and she thinks she's the greatest thing to happen in the twentieth century, too."

"She doesn't sound like my kind of person," I said.

"Oh, don't worry, she wouldn't even notice you, unless you were something fantastic like a rock star or a foreign princess."

"So, I guess I'd better accept the fact that Melissa whats-her-name won't notice me," I said.

"You won't miss much," she said, giving me her tinsel-mouth grin again. Of course, there *is* O.P. who hangs around with her, and he is too much. He's gorgeous—six two, big dark eyes, and lots of muscle. I mean, wow! But Melissa doesn't let him out of her clutches ever."

"Do you have a boyfriend?" I asked.

She looked down at the ground. "Sort of," she said.

"What does that mean?"

"It means I'm crazy about him, but he doesn't even notice I exist."

"I see," I said, thinking this over. One look at her downturned mouth made me feel sorry for

Laurie. "I guess some things are easier at an all-girl school."

"It's OK as long as you're not too fussy," she said. "There are plenty of creeps and weirdos hanging around, but I'd rather keep waiting for Gary—"

"I'm not so desperate that I'd take a nerd or a weirdo," I said, laughing.

Just then there was a crashing on the path ahead, and the shiny purple of my grandmother's warm-up suit appeared, moving quickly toward us.

"Why, there you are," she called, jogging to a halt. "I was getting worried about you. I decided that nobody, but nobody, could take that long to run one mile. I thought you must have broken a leg or something."

"Sorry, Grandma," I said. "I met someone who's going to my new school, and she was filling me in on all the details."

"Well, that's nice," my grandmother said, beaming at Laurie. "I'm glad you'll know someone, and I suppose she's told you which courses and teachers to sign up for."

"Not exactly," I said. "We hadn't gotten around to discussing classes." And I smiled knowingly at Laurie.

"Why don't you invite her over this afternoon, and she can help you plan a schedule—if you're free that is—what is your name, dear?"

"Laurie Wilson, ma'am," Laurie said.

"Marylou Wilson's granddaughter?"

"That's right," Laurie said. "Do you know my grandma?"

"I most certainly do," Grandma Beth said. "She's in my exercise class, and she beats me at tennis. Are you a fitness buff like your grandmother?"

"Not exactly," Laurie said. And I smiled to myself. So that gave us another thing in common. We each had an overly healthy grandmother. I was lucky that I had made a friend so easily, and what's more, a friend who seemed to be exactly like me!

Chapter Five

Already I had learned an important lesson. I had learned that being sneaky pays! If I hadn't decided to cut out half a mile of jogging and creep through those bushes, I'd never have met Laurie. That turned out to be a really lucky break for me. Now I wasn't dreading the first day in a big new school nearly so much. She had promised to meet me on the corner and walk to school with me. She had filled me in on which teachers to choose and which to avoid like the plague.

"By all means steer clear of Mrs. Hollister for English," Laurie advised. "All she talks about are her poodles, and she makes you address envelopes for the ASPCA all the time. You don't want Mr. Demetri for chemistry. He can barely speak English, and he pops quizzes all the time. Avoid Mr. Tanaguchi for PE: he thinks he's running an army base and makes you do extra push-ups if you so much as giggle during roll call."

I learned all this and much more at Laurie's house on Sunday afternoon. Instead of coming to Grandma's, she invited me over there, and I discovered another thing we had in common. She liked to eat junk food and lots of it. We made popcorn together, baked a cake with chocolate frosting, and then decorated it with sprinkles, chocolate chips, and M & M's. It tasted as heavenly as it looked.

In the late afternoon I learned that Laurie had another thing going for her. She had a sister who was a senior and one of the best friends of the famous Melissa Anderson. I met her sister when we were up in Laurie's room, going through her record collection and clothes. We were discussing whether miniskirts were here to stay when the door burst open and in swept this gorgeous creature with lots of make-up, eyelashes that swept right down over her cheeks, and blond hair feathered back without a strand out of place. She saw us sitting there and looked surprised. I expected her to say, "Oh, who's this?" and immediately decide she liked me. And then through her I could get to know this important Melissa girl.

While I was thinking all this, she started bustling around the room, looking at us as if we were bugs on the floor. "Would you two creeps mind clearing out of here while I get changed? I'm in a hurry, and Danny's waiting out in the car." Her voice was as sweet as the cake we had just made—as if she were talking to three-year-olds.

"This is my sister, Patricia," Laurie said to

me. "I share a room with her, unfortunately. Patricia, this is Stephanie Fenton, who's just moved into town from New York City."

Patricia looked about as interested as I normally look while watching a detergent commercial. "Oh, hi," she said. "What year are you?"

"Sophomore."

"Oh," she mumbled and started taking clothes out of her closet. "Now would you both go!" she called over her shoulder.

"It's my room, too," Laurie said.

"It's totally boring having to share a room with a younger sister in the first place, and I need to get changed. I am definitely not stripping in front of a complete stranger. Now please get out."

"Come on, Steph," Laurie said. I followed her to the door. So much for Patricia instantly deciding I was an interesting person. If everyone else had the same reaction to me—if Melissa had the same reaction to me, I was in for a really fun six months.

I don't know why, but secretly I couldn't help hoping that I'd meet this Melissa somewhere special—perhaps in music class—somewhere where she could immediately see my talents and like me for them. Then everyone else would like me—even Patricia. It wasn't that I particularly wanted to be friends with Melissa Anderson; she didn't sound like the sort of person you would want to be friends with. It was just that I knew enough about life to know that if you got in with the right people, everything else would go right.

I thought about this again as I got ready for school on Monday. *It's got to be different this time*, I thought, feeling that my whole life depended on it. *I can't go through these six months being a nobody. I've got to prove to myself that I can be a somebody if I want to.* Then I made another resolution. *And above all, I've got to watch what I say. No more getting nervous and saying the first thing that comes into my head. No more being rude by accident. I can't afford to make any enemies here.*

I took extra care with my appearance that first day. I sorted through the few clothes I had, trying to decide what to wear. After trying on and discarding several outfits, I settled on a big, bright green sweat shirt and jeans. It was a very happy sort of color, and it made my hazel eyes sparkle. It was a new experience putting on makeup for school—after years of nothing but a scrubbed face and clean hair tied back with a green ribbon. In fact, I kept looking around guiltily, half expecting to hear my mother saying, "You take that stuff off your face right now, young lady."

I decided my cheeks looked too pale against the bright green sweat shirt, and so I put on some blusher. Of course, I put on too much and looked like a clown with bright red circles on my cheeks—I had to take it all off again. By the time I had cleaned off the mascara where it smudged around my eyes and fixed my hair back with barrettes, there was hardly any time for breakfast, which really didn't matter because breakfast consisted of a revolting hot, whole wheat mess with real maple syrup on top. I didn't have much of an appetite, anyway, with all the butterflies in my stomach. I raced out of the house, waving goodbye to Grandma, who was getting ready to go jogging.

I had to run to meet Laurie on the corner, and by the time I got to school, my cheeks were glowing as if I had left the blusher on after all.

As we crossed the school yard, Laurie said, "When we get inside, go to the office on your right. Someone there will tell you whether you have to see the vice-principal or dean of students first."

Just then, a boy yelled out something and ran across the yard, brushing against Laurie and sending her papers flying.

I was about to shout something insulting at his back but remembered my resolution and bit my tongue at the last minute. I bent down to help Laurie pick up her papers.

"Well, of all the rudeness," I said to her as I handed her the scattered papers. "Doesn't anybody have any manners around here?"

Laurie was still staring after him. His hair was cut extra short, in a new-wave style, and he was wearing the tightest of tight black denims with a decorated denim vest. Laurie had this strange expression on her face, not at all the look of someone who had just been insulted.

"That was Gary," she murmured. "Isn't he wonderful?"

I decided that, although Laurie and I were alike in some ways, our taste in boys was not exactly the same. I made a quick note not to let her help me get a boyfriend. We walked up the

36

front steps and went inside. We said goodbye to each other, and she floated away to the left.

As I watched her disappear, my panic began growing. I had been at the same school since I was eight years old. My mother had taken me then and introduced me to the principal. Here I was, not only going to a new school but starting school late, when everyone else already had settled in. I had been looking forward to the freedom of being my own person, but I sure could have used my mother beside me right then.

What would I say when I went into the office? Who would I say it to? What if I got lost? What if there was only room in Mr. Tanaguchi's PE class and he made me do extra push-ups every day?

Luckily my panic didn't last long. A friendly looking lady came out of the first office just as I shut the door behind me, and she took care of everything for me. She even seemed to be expecting me. "We already have your records transferred from Saint Catherine's," she said. "If you'd like to go upstairs to Mr. Goodman's office on the second floor, he'll help you with your schedule."

I headed upstairs. The hallway was full of hurrying students. In fact, it was rather like trying to filter in to the expressway at rush hour. Carrying the envelope containing my records, I joined the line going upstairs. A boy ran past and fought his way between the up and down lines to get somewhere in a hurry. I only got a quick look at his back, but I saw that it was Laurie's dream boy, Gary, again.

37

He must always be in a hurry, I thought, *or maybe he's in training for the Olympics.* I was so caught up in thinking about Gary's rudeness that I forgot where I was going. Before I knew it, I was in a flood of students heading up the stairs to the third floor. I immediately stopped in my tracks and turned around—easier said than done in the mad rush to beat the late bell! The girl behind me—who was looking over her shoulder to talk to a friend—bumped right into me as I made my abrupt about-face. We crashed together—hard. As I said "ouch" and started to apologize, she lost her balance and fell. Worst of all, she was wearing a miniskirt, and as she fell backward, her skirt went flying up to her waist. She was wearing panty hose, of course, but it still looked pretty clumsy.

I was about to complete the apology that I had started, but she began yelling at me as her friends helped her up. "What are you—a total loser? Can't you even walk straight, or are you high on something?" Her face was scarlet, and if looks could kill I would have fallen down the stairs and broken my neck.

I looked at her calmly, although I could feel my knees shaking inside my jeans. "Why do you think I'm high on something?" I asked icily. "I'm not the one who fell over."

Everyone on the stairs had stopped moving and talking except for one person behind me who laughed. The girl flashed him a look that made the laugh stop instantly. "You would have fallen over, too, if some klutz had bashed into you!" she yelled, gathering up her purse and books.

"If you'd been looking where you were going and not turning around to talk, you'd have seen me," I snapped back. "I just got a little lost and had to turn around."

"Well, you're a lot lost," she said coldly. "Most people at this school know their way around enough to stay out of my way." Then her eyes narrowed as she looked at me. "Who are you, anyway? Some new kid?"

"I was sent here by the CIA to investigate possible Russian spies," I said and started to walk past her. Then I saw Patricia coming down the stairs toward her. "Oh, Melissa, what happened?" she cried.

"We got some wise-guy new kid" I heard her say. "Find out her name for me."

Melissa! I thought with horror as I walked to the vice-principal's office. Five minutes in a new school, and I'd already blown it. I had knocked over Melissa Anderson, and then I was rude to her. I might just as well have thrown myself off the roof right then. Maybe I could hide in Grandma's attic for six months, I thought, and Laurie could bring me food—a little ice cream occasionally. No, Laurie probably wouldn't bring me food because I had been rude to Melissa. Probably nobody would ever talk to me again.

The vice-principal was very nice. He was a young man who told me to call him Ted. "All the students do," he said. This was a shock after having gone to a school where the vice-principal had been at least three hundred years old and would have had a heart attack if anyone had ever used her first name. We called her Mighty Mouse, but that was behind her back, of course. Ted was really helpful about finding me nice teachers and even got me into advanced chorus. He encouraged me to sign up for a computer course. This was a whole new world for me. At Saint Catherine's they hadn't even heard of computers, except in science fiction books. The idea that students could actually sit and program their own computers was something I had never dreamed of.

"Very useful," Mr. Goodman, or rather Ted, told me. "Your generation is going to have to become expert in computers. There won't be many jobs for people who haven't some knowledge of operating a computer."

So I felt really excited when I went along to the computer lab in fourth period, excited and scared, too. Everyone would know how to use a computer but me. They were already two months ahead of me. I'd probably push the wrong button and make my computer explode or erase a program or something else terrible.

The teacher looked just like a mad scientist. His hair stood up in gray tufts, and he peered at me through thick, rimless glasses.

"So, you've just arrived, eh? Where from?" he asked me in a scratchy voice. When I said New York City, he looked as excited as if I'd just said Oz.

"Oh, that's wonderful, it really is," he babbled. "Such a lively place, New York. Such lively minds come from there. Let's see if you have a lively mind, shall we?"

He spoke so fast I was pretty sure I didn't have a lively mind, but I wasn't going to let him find out too quickly. My mind was feeling more unlively than usual, having gone through a lot of stress in the past few days. I only hoped he wouldn't ask me to solve anything that first day. He led me to my own Apple and sat me down.

"The other students have all been working at this for a couple of months," he said, "but it doesn't matter because the book is self-paced. I'll send over my aide to get you started, and then you're on your own."

I sat staring at the screen and strange keyboard, feeling too scared to touch it. I was just wondering whether I would ever dare turn it on when a boy came up to me. He pulled up a chair and sat beside me.

"Hi," he said. "Mr. Wagner wants me to show you how to get started."

He smiled—the most wonderful smile I had ever seen. Even Michael Jackson didn't have a smile like that. All I could do was stare at him like a dummy.

"Are you new?" he asked. His smooth, rich voice complimented his wonderful dark hair and big brown eyes. I felt like a bowl of Jell-O, but I managed to nod in answer to his question.

"My name's Oliver Pfeffelfinger," he said, looking at me seriously.

My lips started to twitch. "Sure," I said.

"You don't believe me?"

"Of course, I believe you," I said. "Oliver Pfeffelfinger, eh? Well, I'm the queen of Sheba."

"Nice meeting you, Queen," he said and stood

up immediately. He had already started toward another student as he added, "The machine switch is here. I guess you can figure out the rest from the book."

I sensed his sudden coldness. Now I felt cold, too. Surely he had been teasing me, hadn't he? I mean, nobody could really be called—then I heard Laurie's voice in my head, saying clearly, "Of course, there *is* O.P. He's gorgeous—big dark eyes and lots of muscle."

I could have kicked myself. I wanted to yell after him, "I'm sorry, I made a mistake, I thought you were putting me on—" But it was too late. O.P. had already gone. He was on the other side of the classroom, working with someone else.

I gave a big, big sigh and switched on my Apple.

"So, how did it go?" Laurie asked, running to catch up with me as I walked out of the gates. "Did you get the teachers I told you, and did you meet any cute boys?"

"I had a wonderful day," I growled, staring straight ahead and kicking up leaves savagely. "You will be amazed and impressed to hear that in my first day at school I succeeded in knocking over Melissa Anderson and laughing at O.P. They both know who I am all right, and they both hate me. Can there be anything else left to go wrong?"

Chapter Six

"You can't stay locked up here for the next six months, that's for sure," my grandmother said. We were sitting in her living room drinking peppermint tea. Normally I would have gagged on peppermint tea, but right then it felt hot, sweet, and soothing. There was a roaring fire in the fireplace, and the clock on the mantelpiece was ticking deeply and steadily.

I had told her the whole, painful story because I was feeling so down. I suppose I was tired after my long day at a new school, having to find my way between classes, talking to new kids and teachers. On the way home I had realized that my parents were at that moment on a plane to Saudi Arabia, out of my reach, unable to come even if I had needed them. And I did need them badly. It might have been true, as Grandma said, that they had sheltered me and overprotected me, but sometimes that overprotection felt good, and, boy, did I want it then. I wanted my mother to say, "Don't worry, Stephanie, baby, I'll get Dad to straighten things out. Why don't you sit down and have another bowl of ice cream."

Grandma's sympathy was slowly helping. The combination of the comforting room and the tea was beginning to make me feel human again. Grandma had even hugged me when I cried. But she had also laughed when I told her about my mistakes. And that kind of sympathy I could have done without. She didn't understand why I wanted to pretend I had broken a leg and couldn't go back to school anymore.

"You can't expect everything in life to go smoothly," she said. "It takes time to fit in and make new friends. Just because you said the wrong things to two people hardly matters in a school of five hundred kids, does it?"

"Of course it matters," I growled. "Those were only *the* most important people in the entire school. If they don't like me, nobody will."

"Oh, come on," Grandma said with a little laugh. "Do you really think that two people can have so much power that they can say, 'Don't like this girl,' and the whole school will obey?"

"Well, not quite like that," I admitted, "but they *are* the popular ones. If they don't like me, I'll never be in with the popular group."

"Is that such a bad thing?" Grandma asked. "Just because people are popular doesn't necessarily mean they're the nicest people to know, does it? I can remember when I was in school, popular girls were really stuck-up. But I still wanted to be like them—cut my hair and wear

44

a flapper outfit. Of course, my mother wouldn't allow me to, and I thought everyone else would laugh at me for being so old-fashioned in my long skirt and my braid."

"And did they?"

She shook her head. "No—it turned out there were a lot of parents who wouldn't let their daughters dress as flappers. We formed a sort of club—an antifashion club."

"That wouldn't work now," I said bitterly. "Anyone who is not in fashion is weird."

"What I'm trying to say, Stephanie, is that just because you aren't in with the popular crowd doesn't mean you can't have a good time. That Laurie you met yesterday is a nice girl. I bet she hasn't stopped talking to you because you said the wrong thing to this Melissa person."

"Well, no, but—"

"No buts. You'll find there are a lot of Lauries around, and you'll have a good time with them. Now cheer up and eat that muffin before it gets cold."

I sighed and bit into the muffin. It was still warm, and the melted butter oozed into my mouth along with homemade jam. How could I explain to my grandmother that things were different today? How could I tell her what I really felt—about my dream of having a fresh start and making it this time. I longed to be one of the kids the other kids looked up to, so that everyone in school would know my name, everyone would make a place for me to sit in the cafeteria and point me out to newcomers. Now it seemed that the only reason I would be pointed out was to warn other people to stay away from me.

I was just thinking of going to bed and having a really good, uninterrupted cry when the phone rang. It was Laurie, and she sounded excited.

"Hey, have I got news for you," she said.

"Let me guess—O.P. and Melissa eloped together and won't be back."

"Better than that. Didn't you tell me that you liked to sing?"

"Sure, but—"

"My sister just came home and said that the play we're putting on this year is *Grease*! You could try out. Maybe you'd get a lead—"

"With my luck I'll insult the director, knock the leading man off the stage, and set fire to the theater all in one move," I said.

Laurie laughed. "But just think," she said, "if you get the lead in the play, it wouldn't matter if Melissa liked you or not. You'd be a somebody without her—and I bet O.P.'s group will play for the musical—"

"He has a group?"

"Does he ever! He's the drummer, and the whole group is totally terrific! Of course, I may be prejudiced because the lead guitarist does happen to be named Gary Jones. But just think, if you got the part, I could come and visit you every day in the theater, and then maybe Gary would finally notice I exist!"

"I'd like to help," I said, "but with my luck I have as much chance of getting a good part as I do of getting a date with O.P."

"I thought you were supposed to be a good singer," she said fiercely.

"Well, I think I am, but—"

"If you're as good as you say you are, you'll get a part, won't you?" she cut in. "Now, I don't want to hear any more excuses. You'll go and try out for the show if I have to drag you there myself!"

The thought of trying out for a part in a musical made me feel more hopeful. Although part of me was scared about the possibility of running into Melissa and her friends at the tryouts, the other part of me was busy writing a daydream in my head in which I sang so well that when I had finished, everyone stood up and applauded. The daydream expanded itself nicely so that Melissa Anderson also tried out for the part but didn't sing nearly so well. And as I walked away from the stage, I overheard a student saying, "We all thought Melissa would get the part, but that was before Stephanie showed up at school." O.P. would be waiting at the bottom of the steps, stunned by my talent. "Let's forget about that silly misunderstanding," he would say. . . .

Even though it was only a dream, it kept me going for the two weeks until the auditions. One day, right before the auditions, I nearly had a fight with my grandmother. She had gotten me to walk to the store with her. She walked everywhere, even when the weather was terrible, even though she had a perfectly good car sitting in the garage. She wanted me to go along for the exercise and to help her carry bags.

She did her grocery shopping in a funny old corner store in the middle of town, even though there was a Safeway only a few minutes away. The store was like something out of a museum. A little old man with a bald head and a white apron cut slices off a big round of cheese and then weighed it out on a brass scale with weights. The store smelled of coffee and spices and salami, and I'm sure the good smells made people want to buy more. Grandma had bought up about half the store—the healthy half. They did stock candy bars, too, but she ignored my suggestion that we were out of Snickers. She had just loaded me down with two very heavy bags when a friend of hers came into the store.

"Oh, Louise," Grandma called, "this is my granddaughter I was telling you about. Stephanie, this is Mrs. Patterson."

The other woman smiled at me. "How nice to meet you, dear," she said.

"So, where is Charles today?" my grandmother asked innocently.

"He's right outside in the car," Mrs. Patterson said. "Why don't I introduce the young people right now?"

"Why not?" my grandmother said. "The sooner Stephanie makes some friends the better."

I found myself being dragged outside to a waiting VW bus. A boy was in the driver's seat, reading something. Mrs. Patterson tapped on the window, and the boy rolled it down.

"Charles, this is Mrs. Fenton's granddaughter,

Stephanie. She's just moved here. You remember, I mentioned her before."

The boy stared at me. "Hi," he mumbled so that I could barely hear it.

"Why don't you get out of the car and meet Stephanie properly," his mother commanded.

"Oh, Mom," the boy said and sighed. He climbed down, and we stood looking at each other stupidly. There was nothing worse than being introduced to a boy by his mother. My first reaction was that he summed up my feelings about myself—ordinary. To start with, he was wearing glasses. He was very tall and skinny, and he had sort of dark brown hair like mine. He didn't have an ugly face, I mean his ears didn't stick out and his eyes weren't crossed or anything and he didn't have warts on his nose, but it was the sort of face you'd walk by in the school halls and never notice—too much like me.

My second reaction was that this was the boy that Grandma had mentioned to me when I first arrived. So this was the kind of boy that she wanted me to get in shape for! Oh, leave it to grandmothers. Even Grandma Beth was old-fashioned when it came to boys. I certainly was not going to jog and diet just so I could catch this one's eye.

"I asked you to say hi to Stephanie properly," Mrs. Patterson said again.

"Hi, Stephanie p-p-properly," he said.

Great, I thought. *He stutters, too.*

"I think it would be nice if you two kids got together and you helped Stephanie find her way around school a little," his mother said.

"It's OK. I know my way around pretty well," I said quickly.

"She knows her way around," Charles said almost at the same time.

There was an embarrassing silence.

"Mom, I have to get home and finish that report," Charles said at last.

"Yes, I suppose we really must be moving on," his mother said. "It was so nice to meet you, Stephanie—do drop by sometime." Her voice was oozing with hope.

"Thanks," I mumbled.

The moment the VW bus disappeared down the street my grandmother exploded. "Stephanie, how could you be so rude! No wonder you don't make many friends. You've never had a chance to meet boys before, and I take the trouble to find a nice boy for you—"

"One who wears glasses and stutters," I muttered. "And, anyway, didn't you see that he didn't want to meet me any more than I wanted to meet him? You can't throw people together and expect them to like each other instantly. When I finally do meet a boy, I'd like him to be my choice, not somebody else's, and besides, Charles would not be my number-one choice."

"And what's wrong with him?" my grandmother snapped. "He is a very nice boy. You could do a lot worse than Charles."

"I expect he *is* a very nice boy," I said. "But he's not my idea of Mr. Wonderful."

"I am not trying to arrange a marriage," Grandma said. "I thought you needed some friends. Let me tell you, young woman, if you

50

set your sights too high, you'll end up as a snob with no friends at all." Then she started walking briskly down the street ahead of me.

"Look, Grandma, he didn't like me either," I called, running to catch up with her. "And I'll make my own friends in my own good time. But, please, don't go trying to fix me up with any more nice boys!"

We hardly spoke all evening. I went to bed hurt and angry. Why couldn't I ever say what I was feeling to grown-ups? Why couldn't I explain to Grandma that there was nothing really wrong with Charles? I wouldn't have minded having him as a friend, it was just that I saw the way he looked at me, and I didn't want the embarrassment of having him turn me down first. Also, I had a clear idea in my mind of what my first boyfriend should be like—and he didn't look like Charles.

Chapter Seven

Unfortunately my Mr. Wonderful looked a lot like O.P. Every day in computer class was torture. To watch him walk up and down the aisles, bend over some girl to help with her program, whisper something to her, and then watch her look admiringly at him was almost too much to bear. When he helped me, it was like being helped by a robot. He sometimes grunted yes and no answers to my timid questions, but most of the time he ignored me completely. Having him near, but far, was so painful that I tried to struggle through on my own rather than call him over to help.

There is no way I can ever get him to like me, I thought bleakly, *unless*. . . . The one big "unless" was the tryouts. If I got the lead in the play, wouldn't O.P. notice me then? I knew for certain now that his group would be playing for *Grease*. We'd have to rehearse together every day, and wouldn't he see then that I was really a very nice person—make that a very nice, talented, and sexy person. . . .

On the day of the auditions, my nerves were totally frayed. Those auditions had come to represent my last straw of hope. Finally the time had come, and I walked toward the gym muttering to myself, "I've got to make it, I've got to make it."

"You say something to me?" a boy asked as I walked past him in the hall. I realized to my complete embarrassment that I must have been muttering out loud.

"Er, no," I stammered, my cheeks flaming.

He gave me an odd look and walked on. The gym seemed jammed with people. There weren't too many boys, but it looked like every girl in the school was there. A worried and jumpy drama teacher was trying desperately to get our attention to make an announcement. His hair kept flopping forward into his eyes, making him stop constantly to brush it back again.

"Let me explain why we're auditioning for *Grease* now even though it won't be performed until the spring. We plan to allow you some school time to work on your parts and want to be able to write your second semester schedules to include this time. So, now anyone who only wants to be in the chorus over on the bleachers, please," he yelled. Quite a few girls and most of the boys wandered over. "And those of you who only want to try out as dancers go to Mrs. Wright in the dance portable." Several girls who looked as if they had just stepped out of *Fame* disappeared through the doors at the end of the gym.

That still left an awful lot of us. I could see O.P. standing talking to his friends, looking cool and confident.

"Now the rest of you listen up," the man yelled on. "What I'm going to do is to pair you off and hear you sing one of the duets together. You all know the songs? I've got some extra copies here."

There was a stampede to get at the sheets. I was somewhere at the back of it. "And if you have a partner to work with, go sit down and practice together in a corner."

This brought snickers, and the poor teacher, who didn't look much older than us, blushed furiously, making everyone laugh all the more. Several couples stepped aside. I looked around hopefully at the boys who were left, praying that someone would ask me to practice with him, but none of them did.

"We seem to have a lot of girls left over," the teacher was saying. "So some of you boys are going to have to work twice."

Roar of laughter again. The poor man couldn't say a thing right.

"Let's pair you off with you—Bob and Tina, isn't it?" He grabbed the first boy and girl he could reach. "And you"—he grabbed me—"try it with—you." He took me over to a boy.

The boy and I looked at each other. It was none other than Charles.

"Oh, hi," he said. "F-fancy meeting you here."

"We seem to be stuck with each other," I said, trying to choke back my disappointment.

"I suppose we'd better go into a corner and practice like he suggested," Charles said. Frankly, he looked as disappointed with me as I was with him. He blinked at me hesitantly through those serious-looking tortoiseshell glasses. "Have you been in many plays before?" he asked.

"Only a few little things at my old school. Nothing worth bragging about. I hope I make this play, though."

Actually my hopes were quickly being dashed. It's just that I knew I could sing really well if I was inspired. One of the songs we could sing was "You're the One That I Want." If O.P. was singing with me, I knew I could really belt it out. But it would be hard to muster up any real feeling for it with this stuttering, skinny boy singing with me. I was sure that Charles was going to blow my whole audition for me.

My gloom must have been written all over my face because Charles was saying, "You thought you'd make it, and then you got stuck with me, right?" He was serious, and then he smiled. The smile transformed his whole face, making it alive and sensitive. Even as he said it, I felt terrible. I had made it very obvious that I didn't want him as my partner, that I felt I had no choice in the matter, and that he was going to hurt my chances at getting a part.

"I'm sorry," I said quickly, "I didn't mean it like that. Look, let's work on 'You're the One That I Want,' shall we?"

He shrugged. "OK with me. I have a good place to practice alone."

We crawled down under the bleachers. It was cozy and private under there. When we started on the song, I got a nice surprise. Charles had a good voice when he sang—a deep, rich tone and no sign of stuttering.

It's not going to be so bad after all, I thought.

The time flew by, and suddenly the drama coach was calling us all back again. A wild-looking boy walked over to the piano and began a few warm-up bars.

"Now, who'd like to be first?" he asked. A couple finally came forward. They didn't sing very well. One by one, or rather two by two, all those hotshot girls and guys got up and sang. All of their voices were disappointing, but the teacher seemed quite happy with all of them. Finally it was our turn. I could hear my voice, loud and clear, strengthened by hours of practice in the shower, echoing down from the gym ceiling and bouncing off the walls. I knew I was singing well. Charles sounded good, too, a bit shy maybe and not so loud as me, but good anyway. They stopped us after the first chorus.

"Thanks, that was fine," the teacher said. He turned to some students sitting behind him. "Nice voice," he said. "What do you think?"

I held my breath. I wanted to make them say, "She's just right for the lead." Then I heard a voice saying, "They're kind of young looking, don't you think? I really don't know if either of them will fit in with the show's image of high-school kids, but they'd be good in the chorus."

I felt ready to explode. *Chorus—what do you mean, chorus? We were good and you know it. We were the best singers all day. Why are you trying to put us down?* But I tried to act professional and mature and kept my mouth firmly shut.

The teacher was speaking again. "OK, Anne. Well, I'll have to think about it. Get their names will you—everybody, listen up. This is Anne Morrison, my student assistant director, in case you didn't know." The girl got up and came down the steps toward us. I knew her right away. She was one of the girls who was with Melissa when I knocked her down. The girl Melissa had been talking to over her shoulder. No wonder she didn't want me in the play.

"What's your name, kid?" she asked Charles. He told her. She turned to me. "I already know your name," she said and began to walk back. "Do you need to hear Sean and Melissa?" she asked the teacher.

He smiled. "No, I don't think so. I've heard them sing often enough, but they have to come to the final tryout on Thursday. OK, kids, we'll try to have the cast list up by Friday."

I turned away in blind anger and stalked out of the gym. I felt someone touching my arm. "Hey, wait for me," Charles said.

"Look, why don't you stay and try out again without me," I said. "You didn't get a fair chance because of me. That group of kids really doesn't like me."

He smiled and shook his head. "I got about as fair a chance as I'm going to get," he said. "I don't know why I even bothered to come. It's always the same here—the same group of kids run the drama club, the same kids assist Mr. Olivetti, and they try to persuade him to use their friends for all the best parts."

57

"And Melissa gets all the leads?"

"You've got it."

"That's just not fair," I said angrily. The door closed behind us, and we stood in the twilight of a clear, wintery evening. The bare bones of trees looked like skeletons against a blood red sky. "Why doesn't somebody do something about it?" I asked.

Charles shrugged his shoulders. "Do what? Mr. Olivetti really thinks he's choosing the cast members. He's an airhead, and he's easily influenced. If you went and complained to the principal, Mr. Olivetti would say they were fair tryouts, and he'd really believe that, too."

"Well, I think that's very unfair," I said. "I don't want to be in their dumb chorus."

Charles nodded. "You don't deserve to be," he said. "You have a terrific voice. Who taught you to sing?"

"I taught myself, in the shower mostly," I said. He laughed. "You're not a bad singer yourself," I added. We were walking across the deserted school yard toward the main gate. A cold wind was playing with piles of leaves, tossing them into the air and letting them fall again. I turned my collar up and shivered.

"Look, Stephanie," Charles said hesitantly, "I know you didn't like my mother trying to throw us together any more than I did. She's always trying to match me up with girls, and I hate it. Do you think you could forget about that whole embarrassing scene and we could start again as though we just met today?"

"Fine with me," I said. "I'm still deciding

whether or not to forgive my grandmother for it."

"What sort of songs do you like to sing?" he asked.

"All sorts, but ballads mostly, I guess," I said.

"I wonder—" he said slowly. "I wonder whether you'd like to hear some of my songs."

"You write songs? How neat."

He looked a bit embarrassed but nodded. "I've written some that would sound good with your voice," he said. "I'd like you to hear them. Are you free now? We could drive over to my house, then I'd give you a ride home, if that's all right with you."

"You have a car?" I asked. If I had needed convincing that Charles was an OK sort of person, the fact that he had a car clinched it.

"It's nothing special," he said. "Just an old clunker, but it does run." Then he gave me a hopeful little smile.

I looked at my watch. "OK, but I can't stay too long. I told my grandmother I didn't know how long the auditions would take and that I'd just grab something to eat when I got back, but I don't want to push it."

"My car's this way," he said, turning down the street. As I watched him unlock the door of a very old Chevy with fins, I was struck by a thought. *How about that! Only two weeks at school and already a boy is giving me a ride home! I must tell Carly.* Then I had another thought. *But I'm not going to tell Grandma, or she'll think that she brought Charles and me together!*

Chapter Eight

Charles's house came as a shock. Because of his pushy mother and his quiet manner, I had convinced myself that he was an only child, and I'd pictured him in a little country cottage with roses growing round the door. But instead we pulled up to a huge house, almost a mansion. And that wasn't all—the driveway was littered with bikes, and loud rock music was blaring out of an upstairs window. Charles winced and looked at me apologetically.

"My brothers are home," he said. "I thought they'd be out."

"Somehow I didn't picture you with brothers," I said. "I pictured you as an only child, like me."

"I wish." He groaned. "But I assure you I have brothers all right, as you will soon find out."

"Look, I won't come in if you don't want me to," I said. "I mean if you're embarrassed or—"

"Oh, no—do come in, please," he interrupted.

"It's just that—well—they're always having their friends over, and they like to tease me—"

Poor old Charles, I thought. *A mother who fixes him up with dates and brothers who tease. What am I getting myself into? He sure could use some help.*

Out loud I said, "Let them tease. I don't mind at all." I gave him an encouraging smile—the first real smile I had given him.

How about that, Grandma, I thought as I climbed out of the car and walked toward the noisy house. *You thought I was so feeble that I wouldn't even be able to make any friends of my own. And you thought I was such a snob, and here I am helping someone who is much shyer than me. But just don't get any wrong ideas, Grandma. He's nice and I like talking to him—I might like him as a friend, but that's absolutely all.*

As we entered the long, dark front hallway, a boy of about twelve shot down at us with some kind of a toy space gun from the landing at the top of the stairs. He shouted, "It's the invasion of the Super Pickles, aaahhh!"

"That's Bobby," Charles said. "Don't mind him. He's a bit weird."

"I heard that," the voice said again. Then, "Whoopee, Charles has brought a girl home with him. Hey, Cliff, Charles has a girl!"

"Shut up," Charles snapped, but it was too late. Another head peered over the stair rail, this one very good-looking with curly hair—sort of like O.P., I noted.

"Way to go, Charles," came his deep voice.

"Following in the old brother's footsteps after all, eh? Want me to give you a few pointers from my vast experience?"

"Get lost, Cliff," Charles growled. "This is just Stephanie, a girl who likes to sing, and I've brought her home to hear my songs."

"Don't you trust him, Stephanie," Cliff called. "That's what he says to all the girls—come up and listen to my songs sometime."

"Don't worry about me," I said. "It's Charles you have to worry about. Get ready to come and rescue him if you hear a call for help!"

I hadn't known until then just how famous my wisecracks had become—even in the short time I had been in Connecticut. As usual I had spoken before I thought carefully.

"Oh, you're the Stephanie with the big mouth," Cliff said, grinning down from the stairs, "the one who made Melissa mad and made fun of O.P.'s name."

"I didn't make fun of it," I said, defending myself. "I just didn't believe it. I thought he was putting me on."

"He was really mad," Cliff said. "He's very sensitive about his name. It goes back to when he was a puny little kid and people used to tease him about it all the time."

"I didn't mean to upset him," I said. How could I have known that someone who looked like O.P. was ever a puny little kid—good old big mouth Stephanie strikes again.

After we were safely inside Charles's room, he expressed delight with the way I had talked to his brothers. "You were great," he said. "You stopped them in their tracks. They would have gone on teasing for hours if you hadn't shown them that you were better at wisecracks than they were. You can't imagine how I hate being teased. I wish I could think of comebacks when people tease, but usually I'm so mad that I only think of the right answer later, like when I'm in the shower."

"It's a mixed blessing." I smiled and then shrugged as I explained, "The words just come tumbling out before I can stop them, and then I find I've made enemies—like Melissa and O.P."

"Oh, so that's why Melissa's friend made it clear she didn't want you in the show."

I nodded, thinking about how Anne had been with Melissa when I'd knocked her down. Sighing, I said, "Well, maybe I wasn't good enough, anyway."

"You were plenty good," Charles said. "You had one of the best voices there. I think you would have gotten a lead if everything had been fair. I can't wait to hear you sing some of my songs."

"You know what?" I said as he picked up a battered old guitar from a corner. "You don't stutter anymore. How come?"

He grinned. "I never stutter when I feel at ease with people—"

"I'm glad to know you feel at ease with me now."

"I would never let you hear my songs if I didn't," he said. "But I think you're my kind of person. I'm really shy about my songs. Most people wouldn't understand them or appreciate them; so I don't sing them in public."

"How do you know I'm not secretly a talent scout for a famous rock group here to steal your songs?" I quipped.

His face clouded for a second, then he smiled. "Because I trust you," he said. "I think I'll sing you this one first."

He sang, hesitantly at first, then with more confidence. I don't know what I had expected—ordinary, pleasant songs, I suppose. After all, Charles seemed like a nice, shy, and very ordinary boy. But the songs were brilliant. The tunes were so catchy that you could hum them after hearing them once, and the words were so moving that you wanted to cry. There was one about a lost child, one about a polluted river, and one about a young couple after a nuclear war. But my favorite was also the most simple. "Who am I?" it went. "Will I ever know?" It seemed to sum up the way I felt about myself, too.

"Will you teach me that one?" I asked.

"Only if you promise not to sing it to anyone else," he said. "It's kind of personal."

"But, Charles, it's good. They're all good, but that one especially. You ought to share them with the world."

"When the world is ready, I will," he said. "But not around our school. They just think of me as good old Charles, the Patterson boy who's useless with a football, Cliff's boring brother. They'd only laugh at anything of mine."

"Charles, they wouldn't," I said. "Nobody could laugh at a song like that."

"You haven't lived around here as long as I have, and I don't want people to hear my songs. So if I teach you this one, you've got to promise."

"All right. I promise," I said.

He started to teach me. It was really easy to pick up, and soon I could sing it on my own. It was just right for my voice—the guitar and I seemed to be one, making lovely full notes together. When I had finished, Charles was looking at me with admiration.

"That's just how I always imagined it," he said. "You know I was going to write off this afternoon and the tryouts as another waste of time, but now I'm not sorry at all that I went. If I hadn't gone I would never have gotten to know you."

In my dreams I had always imagined a boy saying words like that to me. But why, oh why, did that boy have to be Charles?

Chapter Nine

"What's all this I hear about you and Charles Patterson?" Laurie asked me on the way to school the next morning.

"What did you hear?" I asked, surprised, and then started to blush furiously.

So this is what living in a small town is like, I thought.

"Just that you went to his house yesterday," she said slyly.

I wished I could stop blushing. It somehow made me look guilty when, in fact, I had nothing to feel guilty about. "Who told you that?" I asked.

"His brother is going with my sister," she said smugly. "I hear you spent the whole evening in his room."

I was feeling more and more angry at the way she grinned. "Yes, I was in his room, listening to his songs—but only for about an hour or two, not the whole evening. He likes to write

66

songs; I like to sing them. What's wrong with that?"

"Oh, nothing, nothing at all," she said. But she still grinned.

"Will you stop grinning," I snapped. "There is nothing—absolutely nothing between Charles and me. Just because he happens to be a boy and I happen to be a girl, I am not about to marry him or something!"

"Oh, don't worry," she said. "I think it's just great. I mean, if you've managed to get Charles to sing you his songs, why you're practically engaged to him. He's terribly weird about those songs. He's only sung them to one other person, and that was Becky last year. They were going together for a while, but she sang some song of his at a party, and I guess nobody was in the right mood for a serious song, and they all laughed. Anyway, Charles was really upset. He broke up with Becky, and he's been keeping well away from girls ever since."

"He needn't worry on my behalf," I said. "Because I am definitely not interested."

But by the end of the morning, I realized that the rumor was already around the school. People I hardly knew came up to me and said, "Are you the one who's going with Charles?" Then I heard them giggle as soon as they thought they had walked out of my earshot.

I heard one person passing it on to the next. "She's the new girl who's going with Charles— you know Charles, Cliff's weird brother. The one who looks like an owl."

I began to feel more and more angry—angry

that I was being linked to somebody after such an innocent evening and also angry that they were so mean to Charles. Of course he wasn't another Cliff. He wasn't big and muscular and a show-off, but he wasn't a clown, either. In fact, I really liked Charles. I liked him as a friend, but I didn't want people to think we were going together, that we were a couple. I knew what that meant only too clearly. If you were going with one boy, you were off limits to all the rest. If that happened, I wouldn't get a chance for a real boyfriend at all.

It hardly seemed fair. But then nothing that had happened seemed fair—the accidents with Melissa and O.P., the tryouts for the play, and now Charles. All of those accidents pushed me into a role quite different from the one I had imagined.

I felt like a laboratory animal on one of those wheels—no matter how hard I ran, I could never get to the place I wanted to be.

If only I could start this whole thing over, I thought longingly. *If only I could just pretend the last two weeks had never happened, that I could just walk in again as a new person. . . .*

"Penny for your thought," said a quiet voice behind me. It was Charles.

"Oh, it's you," I said. "I don't know if I want to talk to you. Rumors sure spread fast in this school. If I'm seen talking to you again, they'll probably have our wedding date set."

Charles smiled. "That's what it's like in a small town, I'm afraid. They don't have enough real problems to talk about, and so they have to make up gossip. I'm sorry, I didn't mean to embarrass you when I asked you over to hear my songs."

"I know," I said, my voice softening. "And I do like you, Charles, and I'm very impressed with your songs. It's just that—" I stumbled, trying to find the right words that wouldn't put Charles down.

"That you're not ready to go with anyone yet," he finished for me.

"That's right," I said, wondering if he could read my thoughts. "I've only just got here. I've only just met you, and there are a whole lot of people I haven't even met yet. I want to have fun while I'm here—oh, dear." I broke off. "I didn't mean it like that. I didn't mean you're not fun, I just—"

"Look, I know what you mean," he said, "and believe me, I feel the same way. I'm not ready to go with anyone, either. I had a girlfriend awhile ago, and she let me down badly. I suppose I still haven't gotten over it. I like to know where I stand with people before I become too involved."

"Well, you know where you stand with me," I said. "I'm happy to be your friend."

He smiled at me, and I noticed once more how very warm his smile was. He was like a giant teddy bear, begging to be hugged. I resisted the temptation to hug him because heaven knows what the gossips would have said about that!

During the last period, a note was delivered

to me from the drama club. It said, "We are happy to tell you that you have been selected for the chorus—singing only. Please stop by the drama office to make arrangement for your rehearsal schedule."

I took the note and crumpled it into the nearest wastebasket. Selected for the chorus, indeed! Big deal! Big hairy deal! I'd rather die than sing in the girls' chorus and watch Melissa in the leading role.

I stomped home feeling very bad-tempered. Luckily Grandma was out, probably jogging to Hartford and back; so she didn't have to see the worst of my bad temper. Instead, I made myself some peppermint tea, which I was now beginning to like—wonders will never cease—and curled up with the newspaper. It was soothing to read *The New York Times* and to know that the rest of the world existed—that Manhattan hadn't gone bankrupt and that Saudi Arabia hadn't been buried in a sandstorm. A headline at the bottom of one page caught my eye: "Woman Reappears as Twin." I read the story. It seemed that a woman left her family, and everyone thought she had died. But then she showed up again, pretending to be her own twin sister. Her husband believed her and finally married the twin, who was really his own wife.

What a dumb story, I thought. *Surely nobody could fall for something like that. I mean, if I came back and said I was my twin—* Suddenly it was as if fireworks had been set off inside my head! What had I thought that morning? *If only I could pretend the last two weeks had never happened. . . .* Slowly an incredible, totally impossible but wonderful, scheme started to grow in my mind. I had seen how easily rumors spread around school. What if I spread a rumor that I was going to leave Connecticut to join my parents and that my twin was taking my place—only my twin wasn't like me at all. My twin was pretty and successful; in fact, she was already a professional rock singer!

I jumped up excitedly from the couch and began pacing up and down the room. I'd have to change my appearance, of course—Grandma wouldn't mind that too much. She was always telling me to branch out and develop my own style. As for little matters like school records— well, I'd iron out those details later. And even if I was discovered—think what a name I would have made for myself. I could hear the gossip now: "That's the girl who fooled the whole school." It really was worth a try if I dared to do it.

But I really needed someone to help me get the scheme going and transform me into a rock star named—I walked up and down trying to think of a good name for my famous twin. Outside, black storm clouds raced to hide the sun. *Grandma's going to be caught in a storm if she doesn't hurry,* I thought. Then I had it! Stormy! That was a terrific name for a rock star. Close enough to Stephanie but crazy enough to belong to a rock singer.

I wished Carly were there. Carly would love to help me turn myself into a rock star. But Carly was always broke and certainly couldn't afford to visit even if her mother would let her travel this far. I thought of Laurie. But, after this morning, I wasn't so sure she was such a trustworthy friend. I remembered the way she had grinned when she teased me about Charles. Perhaps she had even helped spread that dumb rumor. I couldn't risk telling someone I didn't trust one hundred percent. She might blow the whole thing before it got started. Also, she was Patricia's sister. I obviously couldn't experiment with hairstyles and makeup at her house with Patricia snooping around. Better not use Laurie then. One thing I knew for sure, I couldn't go through with it on my own. Someone had to help me get my hair styled and choose the sort of outfits that rock stars wore. It just had to be Carly. Carly was the ideal person. She knew every intimate detail of the personal lives of rock stars, and besides she loved secrets.

If Carly couldn't afford to come to Connecticut, maybe Grandma would let me visit New York. It was perfect. I would go away for a weekend and come back as Stormy. My thoughts began to whirl. I might have to dye my hair; I'd need a whole new wardrobe. . . .

All of a sudden a loud thunderclap jolted me back to reality. I had several moments of panic and several second thoughts after that. The weather seemed to match my swirling thoughts. The storm rolled in, and growls of thunder came through torrents of rain. I had always been scared of storms and wished Grandma would come back. I continued to pace like a caged animal.

"What are you, crazy?" I asked myself. "You couldn't get away with a dumb scheme like that. It can't possibly work—they will take one look at you with new hair and new clothes and still recognize you as boring old Stephanie." A voice in my head answered, *But if a woman's own husband and children could be fooled. . . . And I know I can act. This will be my one chance to prove it—it will be my one chance to prove something!*

Just then Grandma burst in, soaked to the skin, her gray hair dripping all over her face. "What a rain," she commented. "I almost didn't do my last lap it was so fierce."

What a grandmother, I thought fondly. *Nothing seems to faze her. I bet she'll let me go to New York. I bet she'll even lend me some money to go, and she'll probably even like my new image.*

"You go get changed, I'll make you some hot tea," I said. "Why don't you take a hot shower, and the tea will be ready by then."

"Good idea," she said. "You know, you are becoming quite useful. I bet you never thought of making your mother a cup of tea."

"My mother would die at the thought of drinking peppermint tea," I said, laughing. "But you're right. I never did a thing at home because someone always did it first, I guess. Now, don't stand there dripping, go get changed before I have to nurse you through pneumonia!"

"It will take more than one little rainstorm to

73

put me to bed," my grandmother said. Nevertheless, she went upstairs. While I fixed Grandma's tea, I started thinking how I would be able to pull this off without letting Grandma know the real reason. She would surely think I was being silly and babyish, trying to start over again as my own twin. I would just have to convince her that I wanted a change—a big change. But she wouldn't have to know about Stormy. Only the kids at school would think I wasn't Stephanie anymore.

I waited until she was warm, dry, and had two cups of peppermint tea in her before I started in on phase one of my scheme.

"Er, Grandma—" I asked, "I was just wondering. Do you mind if I pop down to the city this weekend?"

"You mean Hartford?"

"Actually, I meant New York."

"You want to go to New York? Whatever for?"

"Well, I miss Carly—"

"I don't think you should go running back to Carly, Stephanie. Not just yet. You should make an effort to make new friends here. I did try to introduce you to a nice boy."

Obviously that angle wasn't working. Better try another. "Oh, I am making friends here, and it's not that I can't survive without Carly. It's just"—I had a sudden inspiration—"that it's her birthday, and she wanted me to come to her party. And you're always saying you want me to be more independent, and what could be more independent than traveling by myself?"

Grandma looked hard at me as if she were

trying to fish out my real reasons. "As you know, I'm all for independence," she said, "but I don't know what your mother would say—"

"You know very well what she would say," I answered. "she'd say 'Over my dead body!' But she's not here, is she, Grandmother, dearest?" I walked across and wound my arms around her neck. "And you do want me to grow up nice and independent, don't you?"

"Oh, get away with you," she said, laughing as she shrugged me off. "You're not going to sweet talk me into anything. I've been in business all my life, and I'm tough as nails, remember?"

"Does that mean you won't let me go?" I wailed.

"I haven't said a definite no yet," Grandma said. "But I do feel very responsible for you, and I can't let you go wandering around New York by yourself. If your parents ever found out, I'd be a dead duck."

"But if you put me on the train and someone met me at the station and I promised not to talk to strangers on the way—" I begged.

Grandma laughed. "Well, I guess that would be OK," she said. "Shall I call Carly's mother to confirm all this?"

"No need to do that," I said, not too hastily, I hoped. "I was just about to call Carly anyway."

I called Carly as soon as Grandma was safely in the other room watching a detective movie on TV.

"Hi, Carly."

"It's about time," came her familiar voice over the phone. "I'd given you up for lost."

"Sorry, I haven't had much time. I meant to write as soon as I got here, but my grandmother's been making me go running and other horrible things."

"Heavy social life, eh? Tell me about the boys."

"I'll tell you when I see you—and, uh, by the way, happy birthday!"

"You're a bit early, aren't you? My birthday's in June."

"I know. I just want you to celebrate it a bit early this year—like this Saturday, so that I can have an excuse to come and visit you."

"You're coming down to New York? This Saturday? My mom and dad are going away for the weekend, and my sister's in charge."

"Do you think your mom would mind if I came when she's not there?"

"Of course not. She'd be glad to have you keep an eye on my little brother and keep me out of trouble."

"Terrific."

"What do you want to do? Anything special?"

"You'd better believe it. But I can't tell you here. I'll tell you when I see you."

"Sounds mysterious and exciting," Carly said. "Tell me what train you're coming on, and I'll meet you at the station."

"It's all arranged," I told my grandmother after I hung up. "I'm being met at the station and everything."

I felt rather bad about deceiving my grandmother of all people. I knew she felt responsible for me and that she would probably not let me go if she knew Carly's parents wouldn't be there. But it was a case of now or never. I knew very well that if I let my plan sit any longer, I would surely lose my nerve.

Chapter Ten

"OK. What's it all about?" Carly asked as soon as I was standing on the platform. "It sounded like something mysterious on the phone. Are you planning to meet a boy here or something?"

The train journey had gone without a hitch. I didn't get kidnapped or fall out of the window or any of the other things my mother would have worried about. During the hours of sitting and staring out of the window, I was able to polish up my plan a bit. When I thought out all the details, it still didn't seem real. It was rather like a creative-writing assignment I was plotting than something that would actually change my life.

Carly was there to meet me, dressed in typical Carly fashion in black and hot pink. She rushed up and hugged me and almost dragged me out of the station in her excitement. It felt great to be back in New York City, to be part of all the bustle, and to breathe in the good smells of traffic and garbage cans and polluted air.

I told her the outline of my plan, and she almost stepped off the curb in front of a taxi. The taxi driver, in typical New York fashion, wound down his window and yelled at her. Carly, in untypical Carly fashion, did not yell back.

"You've got to be out of your skull!" she yelled at me instead. "What do you know about rock stars?"

"Not much, but you know everything. You're going to fill me in on all the details this weekend."

"They're bound to find you out. You'd never fool anybody. Besides, a new person can't just walk into a school. You have to bring your school records with you and stuff like that."

"I figured that one out too," I said. "I must admit that that was one of the things that had really bothered me before, but now I've got it all thought out. Only the *kids* at school will think I'm Stormy. I'll tell them that my sister, Stephanie, went to New York for the weekend and got sick, and I'd just come back from a tour and needed to get some peace and quiet, and so I took her place for a while. The teachers will still think I'm Stephanie, and the kids will think they're in on a big joke, you know, behind the teachers' backs."

"You amaze me," Carly said. "Is there no end to your creativity? Why don't you put it to good use by writing soap operas or something—not wasting your time on some dumb scheme that won't work anyway. And to think your parents always thought you were a quiet little thing. What will your grandmother say?"

I shrugged my shoulders. "I'm not sure. I don't think I'll let her in on my scheme. I'll just pretend that I felt like changing my style. I'm sure she'll approve of such independence."

"Just don't blame me if you get caught," Carly said.

"I wouldn't do a thing like that," I said.

Carly laughed. "I would, if it were me," she said.

We turned off Lexington Avenue onto Seventy-fourth Street and walked east four blocks to the building on York Avenue where Carly lived and where I used to live. As I looked around Carly's apartment, I felt very strange. It was terrible to know that I was only one floor below my own home and that strangers were living in it now. Carly said they were nice people with no children and they brought home lots of books from the library—so I knew they were hardly tearing the place apart. But it wasn't easy to know I couldn't go into my own room, not even to take a peak at my furniture.

"Well, if you're determined to go through with this crazy scheme, I suppose we had better get started," Carly said efficiently. "We have only one weekend for a complete transformation. And, frankly, to make you look like a rock star in two days is attempting the impossible. But we'll give it a try anyway."

She walked ahead of me into her room. It looked so welcoming and familiar. It was still cluttered and adorned with posters, but something was different, and it took a moment for me to see what it was.

"Hey, whatever happened to Rick Springfield?" I asked. The walls were now covered with a totally different face.

"Oh, I got tired of him. He's too old for me," she said. "Now it's Billy Case who is the love of my life."

"Never heard of him!"

Carly rolled her eyes to the ceiling. "And this is the girl who wants to convince the world she's a rock singer!" she said. "For your information, Billy Case is one of the up-and-coming greats. He's just starting to get really famous, but when he's known all over the world, I'll be able to say that I was one of his first and most faithful fans."

"If you stay faithful that long," I said. "You once said that about Rick Springfield, remember?"

"This time it is true love," she said seriously and walked across to kiss one of the pictures. Then she turned back to me. "Now, let's get started. Where's my notebook? I'm going to make a list of what's wrong with you."

"Couldn't we start with what's right with me?" I asked.

"The list of wrongs is longer," she said and studied me carefully. "Number one—hairstyle— none. Number two—hair color—blah. Number three—clothes—terrible. Number four—make-up—nonexistent. We're going to be real busy," she added, looking up.

"Thanks, you've done wonders for my ego," I

said gloomily. "I never knew you felt this way about me."

"If I've got to turn you into a rock star, we'll have to be realistic about your faults," she said. "I think we'd better start with the hair. I know a place that does great punk cuts."

"I've got to get my hair cut?" I whispered. "I haven't had my hair short since second grade."

"If you want to look *in*, you need short hair," Carly said. "Then, when it's cut, we'll think about changing the color. After that we need to buy clothes and makeup—"

"Hey, hold on a minute. How much is all this going to cost? I don't exactly make rock star's money, you know."

"We'll try to economize," she said. "But I think we should do things right as much as possible. Maybe I can lend you some clothes and makeup, and I have a great idea on the hair. There's a place downtown where you can get a haircut for free because they try out new styles on you. You'd get the latest style, and it wouldn't cost anything."

"What if I look lousy?"

"You'd look different, and that's what you want, isn't it?" she said. She jumped up and pulled on her leather jacket. "Now come on, let's get moving. Even if this is the craziest scheme I ever heard of, I'm going to do my best for you."

"Thanks, Carly, I always knew you were a good friend," I said.

"And I'm only glad I won't be around to see you make a fool of yourself," she added as we went out of the door.

The hairdresser was on a street where my mother would have forbidden me to go. It was all new-wave boutiques and record shops, which were blaring music onto the sidewalks, and all the people we passed were dressed in weird clothes. I began to have serious second thoughts about the whole thing. *I can't go around dressed like that,* I thought. *I wasn't brought up to be a weirdo.*

"Er, Carly—I don't know if I can go through with this," I said as we passed a girl with blue hair wearing a long T-shirt, boots, and nothing else.

"You're not pulling out now," she said, grabbing my arm in case I ran away. "I'm devoting my entire weekend to your crazy project, and you're not going to quit on me in the middle. Now come on, that's the hairdresser over there."

She dragged me across the street to a red-and-black painted storefront that said Prime Cuts.

"Are you sure it's OK to come here?" I whispered to Carly, who looked quite at home. The name reminded me of a butcher shop, and I sure didn't want my hair butchered.

"Of course it is. In fact, it's the only place to come if you want the latest hairstyle."

We went inside. The rock music was so loud that it was almost impossible to talk. The walls were all black except for mirrors with lights around them. The guy who was doing the cutting looked at me, my outfit, and my long, shapeless hair very suspiciously.

"Are you sure you want it styled here?" he

asked. "I don't want any trouble with your mother."

"My mother left it up to me," I said. "I'm sixteen. I'm a big girl now."

"I hope you're right," he said, picking up a strand of my hair and letting it fall again. "I usually give my customers really wild cuts."

"She wants a really wild cut," Carly said firmly.

"If you say so," he said, looking as if the whole thing were a big joke.

I put on a smock and sat down in his chair. He squirted my head with water, picked up his scissors, and suddenly what seemed like feet of my hair cascaded to the floor. What was left stuck up like toothbrush bristles. I wanted to yell, "Put it back, I've changed my mind. Stop right now, and I'll go around with it half long and half short," but I couldn't make my lips move. I just watched in tortured silence as he cut the sides as short as a boy's, leaving the top in longer curls so that I looked like a clothes brush.

I walked out of the salon in a daze. "Carly, it's awful," I wailed, when I had recovered enough to talk. "Look at me. I look terrible."

"It will be fine when it's blond," she said. "Trust me."

Carly led me to the drugstore, and I, still in a state of shock, followed along like a puppy while she bought a blond lightener and toner.

"Now for the clothes," she said. "We'll buy one basic outfit, and I can lend you some other stuff so that you'll never be short of anything to wear. I know a cheap place with all the latest new-wave fashions. Success depends on how you put it all together," she said, blabbering on like a teacher.

On her advice I chose a basic wardrobe of a pair of stone-washed denims with skintight legs that ended about four inches above my ankle, plus some brightly colored tank tops. Then she promised to lend me a minidress and a couple of oversized T-shirts plus a pair of ankle boots that had grown too small for her. Then she persuaded me to buy a clear plastic vest that she said was really going to be "in."

"I hope I'm allowed to wear something under it," I said as I paid for it.

She grinned. "They make clear plastic jeans to go with it, but they cost an awful lot. You wear bikini pants under them, in case you wanted to know."

"Now we just have to change your hair color and play with some makeup. Then you'll be Stormy Fenton, rock star of the future," Carly said.

When we arrived back at her apartment, I was glad there was no one home. I didn't want one of her brothers to see me with my clothes brush hairstyle. I read the instructions on the lightener out loud and Carly mixed it. She poured the green gunk onto my head, and I didn't dare look in the mirror at all until Carly said, "I think we've left it on as long as we dare," and started pouring rinse water over my head.

I stood up and slowly removed the towel from my head.

"Carly!" I shrieked. "What have we done?" My hair was not the lovely blond I had imagined. It was completely white.

"Carly, I can't go around like this!" I said, wailing hysterically. "Look at me. I look like an old woman. My hair's wrecked forever. I wish we had never started this." I must admit I started to cry.

"Relax, will you," she said. "That was just the lightener to take the color away. Now we put on the toner to bring some color back."

"I hope you know what you're doing," I said. "I have a horrible feeling that I'll end up looking like a total freak. Either that, or my hair will come out in thick handfulls from all the chemicals."

She pushed my head down toward the basin again and poured on new bottles of gunk that didn't smell any better than the first batch. After that, she rinsed and shampooed my hair then dried it with a blow dryer. I didn't dare look that whole time. I felt as if I were in the middle of a bad dream. Had I really wanted to change my appearance? I was dreaming of being somebody else—but did I really want to be somebody else, especially somebody with blond, clothes-brush hair?

"OK," Carly said. "You can look now." She made me face the mirror. A complete stranger blinked back at me. The short sides of my hair made my face look much thinner and my eyes looked twice as large. The way Carly had fluffed up the top gave me a halo of tight, springy curls, all in a pretty shade of blond.

"There you are," Carly said. "It looks great. I

knew it would. Now let's put on one of your outfits, and I'll make up your face."

She had just finished giving me purple-shaded, black-lined eyes and bright red lips when we heard someone moving in the hallway.

"That must be Richard," Carly said with a grin. "Let's go out there and give him a shock. I bet he'll flip when he sees you."

"Are you crazy?" I hissed. "I'm not meeting anybody looking like this. Especially not Richard. You know how he always teases me."

"If you're not going to meet anybody, what are we wasting our time for?" Carly snapped. "A new image won't be any good if you stay in your room all the time. Come on, Richard will be a good test. We can see how he reacts to you."

Before I could stop her, she opened the door and bounded out calling, "Hey, Rich, I want you to meet somebody."

In a panic I looked around the room, wondering where I could hide, wondering whether I could be taken for a lamp if I put the shade quickly over my head, wondering if many people survive a leap from a ninth-floor window.

But before I had a reasonable chance to escape, Carly was back, followed by Richard. He looked at me, and I waited for him to say, "Oh, my gosh, what has Stephanie been doing to herself now?" But he didn't. He did a double take, looked at me long and hard, then said, "Well, Carly, your choice of friends is improving. Aren't you going to introduce us?"

"You're not good enough for her, Rich," Carly

said. "Her name's Stormy, and she's a real live rock singer just returned from a tour in England."

"Well, hi there, Stormy," Rich said in his best how-to-be-charming voice.

"I don't know why you're bothering with a little squirt like Carly here. If you'd rather have a sophisticated college man show you around the city, I'd be happy to help—"

"She already has a date," Carly said.

"Why don't you let her speak for herself," Richard said. "How about it, Stormy?"

I fought back the desire to giggle. "It's real sweet of you," I said in my deepest voice, "but I'm sort of here to rest. And anyway, my boyfriend is such a jealous type. He breaks guitars over people's heads when he gets mad at them. He threw his guitar at a fan just because he stared at me too much during a performance."

I heard Carly give a muffled choke, but Richard looked impressed.

"Well, I don't want a guitar broken over my head, thank you," he said. "Nice meeting you, Stormy. And if you ever get tired of the guitar-breaking guy, give me a call."

Then he walked out and closed the door. Carly and I fell into each other's arms laughing.

"I'd never have believed it," Carly said. "He fell for it totally. And he's known you all his life. It just may work after all!"

"I can't believe it myself," I said. "I don't think I ever meant to go through with it. I don't really think I ever believed I could go through with it.

It was just a nice daydream. But now, wow, Carly—I really think it might work. Do you realize that when I get back there, everything will start to happen just as I dreamed it would?"

Chapter Eleven

Halfway back to Connecticut, I began to have serious second thoughts about the whole thing. That was a polite way of saying I went into a flat-out panic! I had really been up when Carly had seen me off at the station. It had been fun to walk through New York disguised as somebody else, watching strangers turn to stare at me.

"I'd never have believed it," Carly said as we found my train. "But I really have to admit that you do look like Stormy Fenton. Thanks, of course, to my brilliant work in creating you."

"Of course," I said. "I give you full credit. Oh, Carly, you're the best friend anyone ever had. In fact, when I'm singing in Carnegie Hall, the first thing I'll say is 'I owe it all to my wonderful friend, Carly Carpenter.'"

"You don't have to go that far," Carly said. "Just help me with my math homework occasionally."

"I'll do your math homework for life," I promised. "That would be the least I could do to repay you for all those neat clothes you lent me—and the jewelry and the makeup and the records."

"Take good care of them, especially the records. They are my lifeblood, you know."

"Don't worry, I'll guard them with my life," I promised. "And if it all happens as I hope it will and I pull this off successfully, you'll have to come up one weekend and see me in action."

"Now *that* I wouldn't miss for the world," Carly said. "And I only hope that the cute boy you manage to land has an equally cute friend just waiting to meet an interesting, creative, and sophisticated New Yorker like me."

Then the train pulled out, and I watched Carly waving on the platform. She looked like the Incredible Shrinking Woman as she got farther and farther away. For the next hour or so I invented wonderful daydreams about everything—how it was all going to be perfect and how all the kids would want to know me, even O.P., and he would say, "You're not at all like your sister."

I was really having fun being the new me. I could tell from the way other people looked at me on the train—the young ones with interest and the old ones with horror—that my new personality was already working. I was wearing one of my new outfits—my stone-washed denims and a black metallic blouse with a deep V-neck and a wide metal bracelet. On my feet were bright pink boots, the ones Carly had grown out of.

This is the first time in my whole life that old people have looked at me in horror, I thought with satisfaction. *I can't wait until Grandma sees me.* That was when the panic started! It was easy to walk among strangers because none of them knew the real me. But to appear among people whom I knew, to try to be somebody entirely different, that was not so easy. I had forgotten until then that I still hadn't outgrown my shyness, that I didn't like to be laughed at or yelled at. What if Grandma was angry? What if she didn't let me out of the house until my hair grew, or worse yet, what if she called my parents?

"Come on," I told myself, trying to calm down. "You know your grandmother. She's a pretty neat person. She wants you to break away from your old image and try new things just as much as you do." But she did have very strong ideas about the right way to do things. She hadn't been as easy to get around as I had imagined— she had been pretty strict about the jogging and the diet.

The horrible sinking feeling in my stomach was still there as the train pulled into our station. My disguise was so perfect that at first Grandma didn't recognize me. I saw her standing on the platform looking worried as she searched among the people who got off the train. That made me feel guilty as well as scared. After all, she had trusted me enough to let me go away for a weekend. Would she understand?

I took a deep breath and walked briskly toward her. "Hi, Grandma," I called brightly.

She adjusted her glasses, then stood staring as I eased slowly toward her.

"Well, what do you think?" I asked.

She continued to stare. "If you are looking for yourself, young woman, I think you went the wrong way," she said at last.

"But I took your advice—I broke away from my sheltered past, and I'm trying out a new personality. From now on I'm going to be Stormy Fenton."

Grandma let a little smile pass her lips. "Stormy Fenton?" she said. "Oh, well, I suppose we all have to go through it. I remember as a teenager I changed my name to Gloria, a movie star I liked. Well, Stormy Fenton, I suppose we had better be getting home. Is that your real hair, by the way, or a wig?"

"It's real. I had it cut at this place where they do a couple of free haircuts every day to experiment with new styles, and then Carly helped me bleach it."

Grandma shook her head. "I just hope and pray it grows out before your folks come back," she said. "I don't think your poor mother's heart will stand it." Then I think she winked at me as she turned toward the car.

"Grandma, you know what?" I ran up beside her. "You're a terrific person."

She turned and smiled.

"And, Grandma," I said. "I've got just one little request."

"And that is?"

"Can we drive home by the back way? I don't know if I'm ready to run into any of the kids from school."

"Aha," she said with twinkling eyes. "I see that Stephanie's still inside there somewhere. Do you think you'll have the nerve to go to school in the morning?"

"I hope so," I said. "I don't want to have gone to all this trouble for nothing. It's just that somehow I'd rather face them all together than risk meeting someone I know this afternoon."

"I wonder what Laurie is going to think of the new you?" Grandma asked as she turned down a narrow side street.

I had completely forgotten about Laurie! I had left one part of my plan undecided, and that was whether or not to tell Laurie my secret. Should I tell her the truth, or should I pretend to be my twin even to Laurie? Of course I couldn't ask Grandma for advice on this one since she didn't know my entire scheme.

I was quiet and thoughtful through dinner but ate quickly so that I could run over to Laurie's. It was only fair that she should see me before the rest of the kids.

I was glad that it was dark so that nobody would notice me. As I walked I tried to straighten out what I was going to say to Laurie. Was it too risky to tell her the truth and let her share my secret? What if Patricia found out what we were doing? I really couldn't make up my mind. The wind hissed and sighed through piles of leaves, and the streetlights threw long, finger-like shadows from the bare tree branches onto the sidewalk. I broke into a run. I just had to get it over with. I'd start off by trying to fool Laurie. After all, if she was taken in, everybody would be.

I stood on her doorstep, feeling nervous and excited, and heard the doorbell echo in their house. Laurie opened the door herself, looked at me hard, then did such a big double take that I almost burst out laughing.

"Oh, my goodness—I don't believe it! I mean, wow! Look at you—I hardly recognized you. It's incredible, what did you do?"

"Pardon me?" I asked, trying to keep the laugh from creeping into my voice. She looked so funny standing there with her mouth open. "Is this the Wilsons' residence?" I asked formally.

Laurie cracked up. "Oh, cut it out, Steph," she said. "It's not Halloween, is it?"

I smiled a patient, sophisticated sort of smile —or at least, I hoped it looked patient and sophisticated; it might just have looked weird. "You must be Laurie," I said. "Stephanie asked me to come see you, to explain everything."

Laurie frowned slightly in confusion. You could tell that she still half believed I was Stephanie but there were creeping doubts.

"I'm Stephanie's twin sister," I said. "I guess I look a lot like her. We used to look exactly the same before I went into show business."

"Stephanie's twin?" she asked. "Are you putting me on? If this is some kind of a gag, Stephanie Fenton, I will personally kill you."

"It's no gag," I said. "I'm Stormy Fenton, Stephanie's twin."

"But she said she was an only child," Laurie said doubtfully.

"Did she?" I asked, laughing. "We don't get along too well, I suppose, and she's been very jealous of me since I started singing professionally."

"You're a singer?"

"That's right, but I don't suppose you've heard of me. I've been over in England for a year, singing with a group called Urban Slime. I came home because I needed a rest, and what do you know, I find that my parents are in Saudi Arabia and someone else is in our apartment. Guess their letter informing me of their plans got lost. So luckily Steph turned up this weekend, and I said to her, 'Wouldn't it be a laugh if I went to stay with Grandma and took your place for a while?' We used to do that all the time when we were kids. You know, play jokes on teachers. I had to wear a blue ribbon, and she had to wear a pink one, but we kept swapping so that they never knew which one they were talking to. Steph thought it was a great idea because she didn't like it here very much and she'd rather stay with her friend Carly in New York and go to her old school."

"Oh," Laurie said. "She didn't like it here. I see. I thought she and I were getting to be pretty good friends. I was planning to take her skiing with us. Well, it just shows you . . . I wish she'd had the guts to tell me herself."

She looked so totally hurt I decided to give in and confess there and then. I opened my mouth to say, "Had you fooled there, didn't I?" but before I could get the first word out, there came a screech down the hallway.

"Laurie! Is that you keeping the front door open? It's freezing in here. For heaven's sake, come in or go out. Who are you talking to, anyway?"

And Patricia, dressed in a fluffy bathrobe with her hair in rollers, appeared.

"Well, who is it, Laurie?" she asked, staring at me as if I had just landed from outer space.

"It's Stephanie's twin sister, Stormy, just arrived in town," Laurie said. "She's going to take Steph's place at school for a while. She's a real live rock star."

Patricia's expression changed dramatically. "Oh, hi there," she said. "I'm Laurie's sister, Patricia. Nice to meet you, Stormy. Why don't you ask her in, Laurie?"

"I'm sure she's pretty busy," Laurie said flatly, making it quite clear that she didn't want to invite me in.

"Well, I guess we'll all meet you properly at school tomorrow," Patricia said. "Everyone will be so excited."

I gave her my best star smile. "Bye," I said, then turned and walked away. I heard the door close behind me, and the smile faded from my face. I should have been very excited. I had fooled both Laurie and Patricia. But all I could think of was the hurt look on Laurie's face. I wished so much that I had told her the truth before Patricia showed up. I guess I had still been angry about the gossip concerning Charles and me. She really was a good friend after all. I wondered whether there would be a chance for me to set things straight. She had made it very clear that she was not at all interested in being friends with Stormy Fenton.

Chapter Twelve

The next morning I felt so sick and scared and excited all at the same time that I thought I would burst. I couldn't swallow one mouthful of breakfast, and I kept running to the mirror, half expecting my long, brown hair to be back in place. It took me about three trys before I could force myself to open the front door and walk down the path. In the end I had to speak very severely to myself.

"OK, Stormy Fenton," I said, "this is it. You have always complained that you've never been given a fair chance in life. Well, now you have it. Now you are a new person, and it's up to you whether you make it or not. If you blow this chance, you'll hate yourself for the rest of your life."

With that I put all my nagging doubts—about whether I could carry it off, whether Laurie would ever forgive me, and whether the new, improved Stormy Fenton really would be a hit—out of my mind and walked to school.

The rest of the day went well beyond my wildest dreams. I had seen before how news could spread in a small town, but this was like an Olympic race. By the time I got to school, everyone knew who I was. Kids who had barely nodded to boring old Stephanie came running up to me as I crossed the school yard.

"Are you that new girl's twin?" they asked. "Is it true that you're a rock singer? Are you planning any concerts while you're here? Do you know any famous rock stars?"

Then finally, on the steps, Melissa herself was waiting, like a queen with her court surrounding her.

"Hello, there," she purred. "I hear you're Stephanie-whats-its famous sister."

"That's right," I said.

"I'm Melissa," she said. "Did she mention me at all?"

Through my head flashed all sorts of fabulous things I could say, but I decided against all of them. My tongue was not going to get me in trouble ever again. "She didn't tell me anything about this school," I said, "except that she hated it. But my sister has always been a bit of a pain."

"You can say that again," Melissa said. "You know, you really don't look like her at all. You're much taller and prettier. Would I have heard of any of your records?"

"I don't really know," I said carelessly. "I've been singing over in England. We're not too big

100

yet. We had a hit called 'Kiss of Death' a couple of months ago. Did you hear of that one, 'Kiss of Death' by Urban Slime?"

"Oh, I think I've heard it," Melissa said excitedly. Again I tried not to laugh. It was so sweet to be in a position of power over Melissa and watch her make a fool of herself, especially since both Urban Slime and "Kiss of Death" did not exist.

"Listen, Stormy, some of us are rehearsing a production of *Grease* here," Melissa cooed at me. "Perhaps you'd like to come along and give us some pointers on our singing."

"Oh, I don't know too much about musicals," I said, "but I'd be happy to come and watch."

"That's great, it really is," she said. "I can't wait to introduce you to the whole gang. They're all *dying* to meet you."

She put so much stress on the word *dying* that that time I couldn't stop myself from smiling. She took my smile to mean that I was happy to have met her.

It was hard to walk away like a sophisticated rock star when all the time I kept wanting to jump for joy. If only I had someone to share my triumph with. If only I had had time the night before to tell Laurie the truth. It would have been such fun to have rushed up to her and whispered, "She bought it—Melissa really believes I'm a rock star. You should have seen the way she was all over me!"

I remembered back to my first day in school as Stephanie. I had bumbled along on my own and gotten lost a lot at first. It was because

101

I had been lost that I had had that accident with Melissa, and that had started me off on the wrong foot. Boy, were things different for Stormy's first day. Kids practically tripped over themselves trying to show me around. I guess they were pretty excited that I was a rock star and all, but they also liked the thrill of keeping a secret from the teachers. Everyone knew that I was supposed to still be Stephanie in the teachers' eyes, and they did everything possible to help me look like this was just another Monday in old Stephanie's life. Little did they know that I really did know my way around.

I was really proud of my performance that day. I listened patiently while the other students gave me directions to my classes and managed to play it cool while kids gawked at me in the halls, obviously too timid to come up and talk to me. But I was rewarded for my part that day on my way to computer class, a reward that made all my doubts and panic instantly disappear.

I was walking down the hall toward computer class when a big hand reached from behind me and took my elbow.

"I'm going to your next class. Let me show you where it is," said a smooth voice.

The voice made all the short hairs on the back of my neck stand straight up, and I turned to see O.P.'s inviting smile. I hoped he wouldn't feel my trembling as he kept hold of my elbow, steering me in the direction of class.

"The word is out that you're the new girl's sister, is that right?" he asked.

I couldn't look him directly in the eyes for fear of giving myself away. No sane girl could have looked into O.P.'s dark, gorgeous eyes and remained steady on her feet. Instead, I looked straight ahead, trying to play my part as the rather bored, experienced Stormy in high school as a break from tutors and the high life of the rock 'n' roll world.

"That's right," I said. "Unofficially, of course. I mean, we wouldn't want the teachers to hear about our little switch."

He smiled. "Don't worry, they won't," he said. "I'm a student aide in computer class. I'll do my best to lead the teacher into believing you still are Stephanie. What's your name, anyway?"

"It's Stormy," I said, just as I had practiced saying it in front of the mirror the night before. "And who are you?" I put a lot of meaning into that, too.

"The kids call me O.P." he said. "My real name's kind of long."

"I love long names," I said smoothly. "People with long names always end up being company presidents and important things."

He grinned, looking for the first time like a little, embarrassed kid.

If O.P. had paid half as much attention to the real me during computer class as he paid to Stormy, I would have been a computer genius in no time flat. Not only did he help me with the class, but he lived up to his promise about deceiving the teacher. "Look who got a new haircut," he said in a voice loud enough for Mr.

Wagner to hear. He turned to me and gave me a big wink.

Boy, was I glad to be wearing a lot of makeup so that no one could see how I was blushing. He bent close to me and my computer for pretty much the entire period. "Listen, Stormy," he whispered to me at one point. "They tell me you're a rock singer, is that right?"

I nodded.

"I have a small combo myself," he said. "I wondered if, you know, you'd like to come down and sing with us sometime."

"I don't know about that," I said—one of the hardest things I have ever said in my entire life. "I'm kind of bored with singing right now. I've been on a very demanding tour of England. I came here for a rest."

"Oh, I understand that," he said, "but come and listen to us, anyway. Just sit in on a rehearsal, and we can go out for pizza afterward."

"Well, I guess it wouldn't do any harm to come along and listen," I said. "And I do love pizza. In fact, I'm pizza starved. They don't make good pizza in England."

"Great," he said. "How about tonight? Meet you after school?"

"OK," I said and pretended to concentrate on my program as he walked away. I had to pinch myself very hard to make sure I wasn't dreaming. Could this really be happening to me, just as I dreamed it would? Could little, shy Stephanie Fenton, who had never really dared to speak to a boy in her entire life, have acted so cool with such a fantastic boy as O.P.? It was amazing, almost as if Stormy had taken over for me and the person doing the talking was not Stephanie at all.

I passed the rest of the day in a dreamlike state. I stared at my books, but all I saw was O.P.'s smile. Teachers droned on, and all I heard was O.P.'s voice echo in my ear, "How about tonight?"

Carly, I thought, *I will never be able to thank you enough. I'll do every bit of math homework you ever have, and when I'm really famous, I'll get you tickets to every rock concert in the world!*

After school I dove quickly into the girls' bathroom. I retouched my bright red lips and my purple eyeshadow and pulled a comb through my blond curls. I stuck on my dark glasses, determined to stay mysterious awhile longer. As I came out I almost bumped into Laurie walking down the hall with Charles. I didn't know what to say, and so I mumbled a hi.

I was about to walk on when I saw Charles's face. He was looking at me as if he'd seen a ghost. Laurie turned to him. "Haven't you met Stephanie's sister yet?" she asked. "She just got here from a tour of Europe or something. She's taking Steph's place for a while."

"S-St-Stephanie's sister?" he asked. "But she said she was an only child. I remember her saying it." A look of incredible hurt crossed his face.

I tried to laugh it off. "I guess I'm an embarrassment to her," I said, "so she pretends I don't exist. You know what my sister is like."

"I do now," he said. "She's a person who tells lies." There was a pause. "So, I guess she won't be coming back for a while?" he asked.

"I guess not," I said, feeling more and more unsure of myself.

"OK. Well, nice meeting you, S-S-Stephanie's sister," he said, turning his back. "You want a ride home, Laurie?"

I watched them go, quite unprepared for the stab of jealousy I felt. It had been bad enough to see the hurt on Laurie's face the night before and to have her treat me like a stranger. Now Charles's face haunted me. I had never really given Charles a thought while I had prepared all this. Charles was a nice boy to talk to, but it was because I didn't want to get stuck with someone like him that I had invented this crazy scheme. So why should I feel so terrible that I had hurt him? And why should I feel so jealous when he offered Laurie a ride home? "In a few minutes I'm going to meet O.P." I told myself very firmly. "I'm going to meet his group, I'm going to get to sing with them. All the things I've ever wanted and dreamed of are coming true—so why don't I feel on top of the world?"

Chapter Thirteen

"Well, Miss Stephanie, or should I say Miss Stormy," Grandma said as I came in on Friday evening. "You seem to have achieved what you wanted with your new appearance. That was an incredibly good-looking young man who drove you home."

"Yes," I agreed and unbuttoned my jacket. It was the end of a whole week of exhilarating evenings with O.P. and his group. It was just as if I'd finally managed to open a door I had been pushing against all my life and had at last achieved the magic place on the other side where I knew I belonged. To sit there for the past week while the whole room throbbed with sound, to watch O.P. at his drums, those drumsticks flying in his hands as if they had lives of their own, seemed all I had ever dreamed of. It was lucky I had told everyone I needed a rest from singing because I didn't know most of the songs they wanted me to sing with them. I wished Carly had been closer because she knew all the latest hits.

But I listened hard as I sat at the practice sessions, and I did my homework while listening to Carly's albums until I fell asleep every night. After every rehearsal we went out as a group, and everybody treated me with so much respect it was embarrassing.

"Is it true that you met Rod Stewart?" they kept asking. "Do you know the Pretenders?"

I bluffed my way through all the questions, feeling smug at the way I had stepped into my new personality. I didn't feel very smug about O.P., though. He asked more questions than anyone and wanted to know all the details of my band and the company I recorded for. We were rarely alone together, but he hung on my arm constantly when we were around his friends.

"So, it's all working out just the way you wanted it to?" Grandma asked, looking at me over her book. I had flopped down on the couch eager to wriggle my feet free of those pointy-toed boots and glad to be away from all those questions for a while.

"Yes," I said. "Well, almost, I guess. . . ."

She closed her book. "Almost?"

"It's O.P.," I said, massaging my toes and sighing. "When he asked me to come to their practices, I thought I had it made. But he really doesn't treat me like a girl at all. I mean, not like a special girl."

"You mean he's not romantic toward you?" Grandma asked.

I nodded.

"Perhaps you're trying to achieve too much too quickly," Grandma said. "Just because you've changed your appearance doesn't mean you've changed the basic person inside. You haven't been around boys much, and I bet it shows. Some girls have practiced flirting since junior high. I'm not saying that's a good thing, but it's probably true that boys prefer girls who are at ease around them. Probably you aren't at ease yet."

"You're right," I said. "I know I'm not at ease. I have to think out carefully everything I want to say, and I have to stop myself from sounding nervous." I couldn't tell Grandma the real reason why I had to think so hard before I spoke. But even without Stormy's personality to keep up, what I was saying was true.

Grandma smiled encouragingly. "Give it time," she said. "Perhaps the young man might find your appearance a bit too extreme. After all, not everybody likes to look at bright purple eyes and red lips."

"Perhaps you're right," I said. "Maybe my appearance does put him off a bit." So the next evening I toned down my makeup and left off the dark glasses. I wore my T-shirt minidress and black fishnet stockings. I noticed as I looked in the mirror, that after a few weeks on Grandma's diet, I really had lost weight and I looked better for it. Now, in that minidress there were no bulges in the wrong places, and my legs in the black fishnets looked long and sleek.

Grandma looked up as I came downstairs. "I must say that's a definite improvement," she said. "You look like a girl again. Of course, the skirt is a little short for my taste, but I dare say I'm old-fashioned."

I could tell O.P. was impressed, too, when he came by to pick me up.

"Heeeey," he said, looking me up and down from my black fishnets to my blond curls. "I see you decided to take a night off from being a rock star to become a girl instead."

Those eyes unnerved me. "Well, it's hard to live up to an image all the time," I said.

"Oh, don't apologize," he said. "I like the look of you just the way you are."

All the way to Gary's house, where the group was rehearsing, O.P. kept glancing across at me, special little glances, sending out messages that made my heart pound.

Finally, I thought. *After all these years of waiting and dreaming and hoping, a boy is looking at me as if I'm special. And not just any boy—the cutest boy in the whole world!*

I got out of the car as if I were walking on air. But once the band started warming up, suddenly it was all business, and I was forgotten while they went into their first number.

"Come on, guys," O.P. yelled at the end of it. "That was kind of sloppy. It's only a week until we have to play at the dance, and we don't even know what we're playing yet."

"I want to do 'Only One More Time,'" Gary said. "I really like that part in the middle where I can do a guitar solo." He picked up his guitar and played it.

"No good," O.P. said. "That song is really a

duet. It will sound weak with just me singing it. It really needs a girl. . . ."

One by one they turned to look at me.

"How about it, Stormy?" O.P. asked. "We can't do it without you."

Suddenly I found myself standing at a microphone, and I didn't feel a bit nervous. Again it was as if Stormy had taken over and she was not a bit scared of singing with a group of high-school kids. I gave it full power, and I heard my voice blending strongly with O.P.'s. I don't ever remember sounding that good before.

Obviously the guys thought it sounded pretty good, too. They clustered round me as soon as I had finished.

"Wow," Gary said. "This group never sounded like that before. That's what we've needed—a girl lead singer! Why doesn't she sing at the dance with us?"

"She's a big star," Pete, the bass player, muttered. "She wouldn't want to sing with a bunch of nobodies."

O.P. came over to me and draped an arm around my shoulder. I felt that shoulder tingling as if electricity were flowing into it. "Look, Stormy," he said, "I know you're supposed to be resting and all that, but would you do it, just this once, just as a favor to me?"

His face was very near mine, and his big, dark eyes were gazing down at me. "How can I refuse," I whispered.

"You're terrific," he said and drew my chin toward him to brush his lips against mine. "We're going to be a smash hit," he said, grinning as he went back to his drums. "We are going to be so famous, we'll get college dates and then—"

"And then—New York—Johnny Carson's show —our own TV series—movies!" Gary yelled.

"Yeah, and then the dope, the booze, breakdowns, suicides—all waiting for us," Pete muttered.

"Don't worry, Pete, we'll dump you when we make the big time, just to spare you all that," O.P. said teasingly.

They were all so excited, like little boys with a new toy, really believing that their big break was just around the corner and I was the magic ingredient that could lead them to it. I felt a quick jolt of fear. Were they expecting something from me that I couldn't give them? Were they dreaming they could make it because I was a star and knew all the right people? What would they think if they found out I was a nobody? I pushed the worries to the back of my mind. "The former nobody, Stephanie Fenton, worried about things all the time," I told myself very firmly. "The new, improved Stormy Fenton never worries about tomorrow."

"What would you like to sing?" O.P. was asking. I was glad that I'd been learning all the latest songs. Now I had a good idea of what they sounded like. We tried some and chose four or five that we liked.

All in all it was a very satisfying evening. O.P. was still very excited as we drove home. "You don't know how lucky it was for us that you came here," he said. "We're going to be a smash hit next Saturday."

He pulled the car over to the side of the road and slid an arm around my shoulder. "But let's not talk about music anymore," he whispered, drawing me toward him.

His kiss was a big shock, especially for a girl like me who until then had only been kissed by aged aunts on her birthday. Like every other girl my age, I had done a lot of dreaming about my first real kiss. It would be a magic moment —a gentle, warm, sweet melting of his lips against mine. But O.P.'s kiss was anything but gentle. It was rough and demanding, crushing my lips beneath his as he pushed me against the seat. It left me breathless and more than a little scared.

"Hey, listen, Stormy," he murmured as we came up for air, "what say we drive over to my place right now? My folks are out for the evening, and we'd have it all to ourselves. . . ."

My first reaction was anger. What sort of girl did he take me for? But then, in a flash, I realized, *He thinks I'm a rock singer; I'm the sort of girl who has been in Europe for a year by myself. Naturally he thinks I'm experienced. Why shouldn't he?*

His lips were nuzzling at my neck and my ear, and in spite of myself, it was getting harder to think straight. I almost wanted to tell him that I would go to his house. Wasn't that what I wanted, after all, to be alone with O.P.? Stormy would have gone without a second thought, but sensible little Stephanie was still lurking inside me.

"Look, I'm staying with my grandmother," I

said to him. "She's very old-fashioned, you know. She gets worried out of her mind if I stay out after twelve, and I guess I have to go along with that. You know, house rules. You do understand, don't you?"

"Sure," he growled, straightening up and re-starting the engine. We hardly spoke all the way home.

It's all the fault of this stupid pretending, I thought sadly. Why couldn't it have been a real first date? Why couldn't I have told him what was really in my heart—something like, "Look, O.P., I like you very much, but I'm new at all this, so please don't rush me." But there was no way I could tell him. I knew only too well that the only reason he had asked me out in the first place was because he thought I was a real rock singer. I also knew that he hadn't looked twice at little Stephanie.

Chapter Fourteen

"Well, hi there, O.P. The name's Melissa, remember. I mean, you haven't spoken to me for quite a while. I thought maybe you'd forgotten I existed." Melissa looked stunning in a strapless black dress, and the gym, decorated with hundreds of paper streamers and paper flowers, echoed with the cheers and whistles of the kids who had just danced to our last song.

We were taking a break, and I was standing on the stage with O.P., basking in the attention, his arm around my shoulder saying for all the world to see, "This star is my girl." The band had all rented black tuxedos and white, pleated shirts with wing-tipped collars. I had decided to go along with that, too. They had managed to find one that was small enough to fit me, and I must admit the black really looked good against my new blond hair. Also the fact that I was wearing a tux like the boys meant that I didn't have to compete with all those girls in their long dresses. Could you imagine a rock star in a frilly dress?

But from the way Melissa was looking up at O.P., you'd have thought I was Miss Universe in my tuxedo! She looked from him to me and back to him again.

"I've been kind of busy," O.P. replied uneasily.

"Yeah, I bet you have," she said with icy sweetness and glanced at me again with her big green eyes. "That was a terrific song you just sang, Stormy. Are you planning to stay with us long? We were hoping your sister would be back soon. We all miss her."

"I wasn't planning on going anywhere for a while," I said, matching her icy tone. "I like it here. It's so peaceful."

Melissa didn't say another word. She turned on her heel and pushed her way back through the crowd.

O.P. had moved away to check something on his drums, and I heard Gary whisper to Pete behind me, "It won't stay peaceful around here if Melissa decides to get her claws in. Did you see that look she gave them as she left?"

"Well, O.P. shouldn't have dropped her the moment Stormy showed up," Pete replied.

Until that moment I hadn't fully realized what I had achieved. For the former nobody Stephanie Fenton to have gotten O.P. as a boyfriend was pretty unbelievable. But to have taken him away from Melissa made it even sweeter.

I bet Laurie would appreciate that joke, I thought suddenly. I found my eyes searching the room. Where was she? I finally saw her, looking pretty but shy, in a soft, flowery dress. She was standing near the punch with a couple of other people, but she didn't look too involved with them.

If only I had let her in on my secret, I thought. *If only I had dared trust her right from the beginning.* What fun it would have been to have shared a knowing wink with someone who knew I was fooling them all! My thoughts did a quick flashback to New York and to Carly. I thought of the two of us laughing as we bleached my hair and of Carly lending me half her precious clothes. *Nothing's much fun if you don't have friends to share it with,* I thought and hurried off the stage to get something to drink before the next set.

It was strange how I kept thinking about Charles. He hadn't been at the dance. I guess dances weren't his style. But I found myself wanting him to hear me sing. His songs and the evening we had sung together kept creeping into my mind. It's not that I really wanted to think about him. After all, when a girl had O.P. following her around all day, who needed a Charles? But however hard I tried, I couldn't stop him from popping into my thoughts. Maybe it was because I didn't really enjoy being the cold, pushy Stormy Fenton and Charles reminded me of my old self. His song kept creeping into my head, "Who am I? Will I ever know? When I find a me to be, I'll be myself again."

I suppose the truth was that I was lonely. Before, I had always had Carly to share things with, and my friends at school had been partners in my all-girl misery. Now I just had O.P. and his group. They were funny enough: Gary was a good wisecracker, Pete had a dry sense of humor, and Ryan was the listener, but it was like being with creatures from another planet. Their jokes were all about a life I didn't really share, and O.P. himself—well, I was beginning to realize that O.P. only liked talking about one thing—and that was O.P. More and more I got the impression that O.P. didn't want to know me because I was me, but because he imagined I knew people who could help him break into show business. He kept asking me things like, "What's Pink Floyd like? Did you ever meet Pat Benetar?" and I just kept bluffing and lying, feeling more and more uncomfortable all the time.

O.P. was very determined to make the big time, that was obvious, but I wasn't so sure he could do it. To be quite frank, I didn't think he had much talent. He had a wonderful smile, of course, which made all the girls melt. He had an OK voice, but it was pretty much like other OK voices, and he had an OK group, pretty much like other OK groups. When it came to talent, I couldn't help but compare Charles and his songs. Charles had loads of talent. His songs had beautiful words and music that would make any singer sound good. But he didn't want to share those songs with anyone. *If only they could trade places*, I thought. *If O.P. tried to succeed with songs like the ones Charles writes . . .*

I hardly saw Charles anymore, and when I

did, he didn't seem to notice I existed. If I said hi he merely nodded and walked past.

I had other problems, too, like fighting off O.P. in the wrestling sessions in his car. I constantly found excuses not to be alone with him.

"What's wrong?" he demanded one night. "Don't you like me or something?"

"Nothing's wrong," I said. "And, of course, I like you."

"Then why do you keep fighting me off? You aren't going to pretend that you are Little Miss Innocent, are you? I know what it's like on those rock tours."

"Maybe that's not what I want," I said. "Maybe I'm looking for someone who's romantic and gentle."

O.P. sighed. "I just don't get you," he said. "You don't really make sense. It's like you're two different people."

"Maybe I am," I said.

We didn't talk about it anymore, but I suddenly wished I could stop my silly game and go back to being me again. But how? Now I didn't even look like Stephanie anymore. The real me was trapped inside a person I didn't even like.

One day I was standing at my locker when Laurie came up to see me. "Do you ever hear from your sister?" she asked.

"Oh, sure, she calls all the time," I said. "She's fed up with New York and wants to come back."

"You should stick around when she comes

back," Laurie said. "That will be fun when the teachers realize who you really are." Then her face grew thoughtful. "Of course, she wouldn't enjoy seeing you with O.P. In fact, she'd be very jealous. Every girl in the school envies you. She really wanted him to like her, you know. Poor Steph—nothing much went right for her here. I can see why she wanted to leave. Tell her I miss her, won't you—even though she did pull a dirty trick on me."

"I'll tell her," I said, wishing that my blond hair were a wig I could rip off. Then I had a great idea. "Look, Laurie," I said, "why don't you come to our practice session one evening? It would be a great chance for you to get to know Gary—"

I didn't get any further than that because Laurie exploded. "Boy, your sister's got a big mouth!" she said, fuming. "Just what else did she tell you about me? The brand of tooth-paste I use? And get it straight that I don't need anybody else's help when it comes to boys. If I can't get him to notice me without your help, then I'd rather not have him at all." She turned and started to walk away. Then she looked back over her shoulder. "Oh, and forget that bit about missing your sister," she said.

I walked away feeling miserable. I thought setting Laurie up with Gary would be a way to get to be her friend again. But she had totally misunderstood me. It seemed there was no way I could ever get my old friends back.

The more I tried, the harder it became. So every girl in the school envied me. Wasn't that just what I had wanted? Funny how things in life get twisted around. At least I was learning something, and one of the things I had learned was that perhaps popular, sexy, and famous were not the greatest things in life.

I was in a very quiet sort of mood when I went to sing with O.P. that evening. Charles's song kept running through my head. "When I find a me to be, I'll be myself again." While the guys were looking over some music, I picked up Gary's guitar and started to sing the song softly to myself. Gradually I became aware that O.P. was watching me.

"What's that you're singing?" he asked.

"It's nothing. I was just fooling around. It's not a real song," I said.

"Well, just sing the bits you have—that chorus bit, 'Who am I? Will I ever know?' Is that how it goes?"

Reluctantly I sang it. I could tell I was heading for trouble. O.P.'s eyes were very bright.

"That's it!" he yelled when I finished. "That's the song we need. We'll get a demo tape made of it and send it to the big record companies. It will just suit my voice. Maybe we'll put in some piano. What do you say, Pete?"

"Just a minute. You can't do that," I interrupted.

"Why not? Is it already recorded? Who owns the copyright?" O.P. demanded. He looked like a spoiled child fighting for his favorite toy.

"A friend of mine," I said. "It hasn't been published. He's not through with it yet."

"Well, write to him and get permission," O.P. snapped. "Tell him we'll make his song famous. I've got to have it."

"I can't do that, O.P." I said.

"Fine," he said, shrugging his shoulders. "If you won't help me, I'll just work on what I've got here and build my own song around it. If he doesn't have a copyright, then it's mine to steal anyway, isn't it?"

I felt terribly angry and guilty at the same time. Charles had made me promise I'd never sing his songs to anyone. I hadn't really meant to sing it, and I wouldn't have if O.P. hadn't overheard me. I had already let Charles down once. Now what would I say, that Stephanie sang his song to her sister who then gave it to O.P.? There was no way of explaining it without making me sound like a rat.

"You can't do that!" I yelled. "The song is not yours, and it's not mine. If you're patient maybe I can get it for you someday, but you can't just take it. If you do that, I'll get my friend to sue you."

O.P.'s eyes blazed. "So you care more about this so-called friend than you do me, is that it? Is that why you keep fighting me off? You've really got another guy who's a big star?"

The guys in the band had moved away uneasily. O.P. was yelling for all the world to hear. I felt pretty embarrassed, too, embarrassed and scared. I tried to calm him down.

"Look, we're only talking about a song that

doesn't belong to either of us," I said. "Just be reasonable!"

"Reasonable!" he yelled even louder. "Lady, you are talking about my whole future. Do you think I want to be stuck in this crummy little town all my life? I want to get somewhere and be somebody. I know I could do it with this song. I've got to have it, and if you cared about me at all, you'd get it for me!"

"I'm sorry," I said. I grabbed my coat and started to walk out of the room. I walked slowly with my head held high even though I was trembling inside. The fact of the matter was that I didn't care about him. Sure I liked being seen with him, and I was proud of having caught the best-looking guy in the school, but I didn't really care about him. I was also pretty sure he didn't care about me either.

It was dark outside. The early winter snow was a fine powder that blew directly into my face. I was cold, and I wished I had worn a hat.

I don't care, I'll walk anyway, I thought, feeling warm tears run down my cold cheeks. *I'm not going back into that room to ask for a ride. They can find my frozen body under a pile of snow for all I care.*

I hadn't gone far when a car pulled up beside me. "Come on, get in," O.P. ordered.

"No thank you," I said primly. "I'd rather walk."

"Come on, don't be an idiot! You can't walk in a snowstorm," O.P. snapped.

"I can do what I like," I snapped back at him.

"Perhaps you'd better realize that. I'm not owned by you."

"Look, Stormy." His voice was softer now. "I'm sorry. I've got a terrible temper, I know it. Please get in. I don't want you to walk home in this weather."

I weakened and climbed into the car, the instant warmth melting the snowflakes that had settled on my hair and eyelashes. O.P. leaned over and touched my hand. "Look, we won't talk about that crummy song again, all right?" he said. "Do you forgive me?"

I nodded, angry at my own weakness. He could be so charming when he wanted to. He leaned over, putting one finger under my chin, and drew my face gently toward him. "Let's kiss and make up, shall we?" he whispered and kissed the tears off my cheeks.

Chapter Fifteen

After I had walked out on O.P., he tried to be really nice to me for a while. I enjoyed being pampered, but I still felt uneasy. I had never been in love or even gone with a boy before, but I was smart enough to realize that something was missing in our relationship. He *was* the cutest guy in the world, I had to admit. His smile could bring every girl within miles running to help him. But when he kissed me, I didn't hear bells ringing wildly inside my head.

So what? I argued with myself. *You'd be a fool to break up with a guy like that just because you aren't madly in love with him. Real love probably only happens once or twice in a girl's entire life. If you're lucky enough to have a truly gorgeous guy to escort you around, make the most of it!*

I was dressing for a big party that Charles's brother Cliff was throwing as I thought about O.P. and me. I wondered if Charles would show up at his brother's birthday party, but some-how I doubted it.

I took extra care with my appearance that evening and settled on very tight black jeans with a brightly striped top, plus Carly's wide, metal-studded necklace. O.P. and I arrived late, and we could hear the throbbing bass of a loud stereo and gales of laughter coming from the house.

"Oh, here they are now. Here's O.P. with Stormy," kids called as if two celebrities had arrived. I must admit that that boosted my ego. Nobody had ever greeted old Stephanie with such enthusiasm.

"I like your necklace," Patricia, Laurie's sister, said as someone put beers into our hands and dragged us into the middle of the crowd.

"Hey, what's this?" O.P. asked, grinning. "Don't tell me your mother allows you to have beer these days!"

Cliff laughed. "I'm an adult, old buddy. I can do what I like. It's you little kids who shouldn't be drinking. But don't worry, my parents are out for the evening. They said they couldn't stand the noise."

Everybody laughed, and we were swept with a tide of people into the living room. It was dark in there, with just a strobe light flickering. It threw unreal shadows on the walls, shadows that twisted and jerked in time to the beat. O.P. and I started dancing. The room was really hot. I took a sip of beer but almost spit it out. Before the next song started, I found myself a Coke instead. But most of the people around me were chugalugging the beer. O.P. certainly was. His dancing became more and more mellow as the party progressed, until he was draped over my shoulders, barely swaying.

"I think we should sit this one out," I said firmly as his whole weight fell onto me.

"Hey, let's you and me go upstairs and find somewhere where we can be alone," he tried to whisper, but his slurred speech was loud enough for all the kids around us to hear.

"I've told you the answer to that one before," I said.

"I wish you'd loosen up," he said. "What kind of rock singer are you, anyway? Rock singers aren't supposed to be uptight."

"I'm going to get another Coke," I said, breaking away from him. "I'll be back in a minute." I watched as he weaved toward the stairs and sat down.

I went into the kitchen and got myself a Coke from the refrigerator. The kitchen contained all the kids who were tired of the loud, smoke-filled living room, and I joined them.

"Where's O.P.?" one of the girls asked me.

"I left him back in the hall, sitting on the stairs," I said.

"A bit worse for the wear?" the girl asked, smiling.

I nodded. "You could say that."

"Poor old O.P." she said. "He and drink do not agree, and he doesn't know when to stop."

"I'd better get back to him," I said and walked back out into the darkness. O.P. was no longer sitting on the bottom stair; so I wandered into the living room again to look for him. A slow tune was on the stereo, and couples were swaying as though knit together. Just inside the door Gary was talking to Pete. They didn't see me come in. I was just going to say something when I heard Pete say, "So he's disappeared with Melissa, has he?"

Gary laughed. "Yeah. They were both pretty out of it, but they struggled upstairs together."

"What happened to Stormy?"

"How should I know? I think he got fed up with her playing hard to get."

"Yeah, O.P.'s not normally that patient where girls are concerned."

"But this girl's special," Gary said. I felt myself blushing. So I really did mean something to O.P.

"How do you mean, special?" Pete's voice came back immediately.

"It's obvious, isn't it?" Gary's voice came through the darkness. "He's not going to let go of her until she helps him meet somebody famous and gets the group launched. He wants her for what she can do for him, nothing more. I mean, she's hardly a Melissa for looks, is she, and she's not that much fun either."

"No, she's kind of quiet. I don't know how she got into the rock business, *if* she really is?"

"You don't think she is?"

"Who knows? She does have a good voice, but she doesn't come across as someone famous to me."

"That would be a good joke if she really wasn't,"

Pete said. "Can you imagine how mad O.P. would be?"

I turned and pushed back out through the crowd, making for the security of the lighted kitchen. I sat down at the table and started shoveling potato chips into my mouth, munching rhythmically to stop myself thinking. So all my suspicions were true. O.P. was only using me, and my star act wouldn't fool anybody for much longer.

More and more kids came into the kitchen, complaining that it was too hot to dance anymore. I saw Pete and Gary come in, too.

"There she is, go and ask her," someone said to Cliff, and to my horror I saw him pointing to me.

"Hey, there, Stormy," he said in an official-sounding voice. "We have a little question to ask you."

Here it comes, I thought. *They're going to ask me if I'm really who I say I am, and it will all come out. Can I go on pretending? Why not just tell them and get it over with?* A great feeling of relief swept over me—how wonderful not to have to live an act anymore. Then I remembered Pete's saying how mad O.P. would be. I had already seen his temper. If they had to know the truth, it had better not be now, not when O.P. was drunk.

"OK. Ask away," I said, trying to sound casual.

"Some of the kids mentioned that you knew Billy Case," Cliff said. "Is that true?"

I felt all those eyes looking at me. I gulped. "Sure it is," I said. "I know Billy Case."

Cliff's face lit up. "Great!" he said, "That's just what we needed. You're going to be our guardian angel, Stormy."

I must have looked completely bewildered because Cliff laughed. "Don't look so scared about it," he said. "Let me explain. You've probably heard that our class wants to install an elevator so that handicapped kids can get to classes on the second and third floors at school. Well, we need a lot of money, and car washes and bake sales aren't really enough. This is where you and Billy Case come in. Someone heard Billy Case comes from Hartford, and we thought that you could ask him to come and give a concert for our elevator fund. We'd like you to sing, too, of course. Maybe you guys could do a duet. How about it, Stormy?"

They were all staring at me, all those hopeful eyes. I could feel the sweat trickling down my back.

"Well, I don't know," I said shakily. "I mean, Billy's getting to be a big star now. He might not want to do something like this."

"That's what we thought," Cliff said. "We were all saying that nobody as big as Billy Case would come out to a crummy school like this, even if it was for a good cause. So when we heard that you knew him, we thought—hey, he might just do it as a special favor for a friend. So you *will* ask him, won't you, Stormy?" He came over and put his arm around me. "You'll make him come for us, won't you?"

I looked up, and there was Gary, staring at

130

me across the room. I took a deep breath. "Sure," I said. "I'll make him come."

As soon as possible I slipped through the crowd and out through the back door. It was a wonderful, clear night. The full moon was shining on the snow so that the whole world looked as if it were made of silver. I walked over and leaned my forehead against one of the posts on the porch.

"Now that's an interesting way to cool down," said a voice behind me. "Most people would put ice cubes in their drinks."

I spun around, and there, swinging gently on the porch swing, was Charles.

"What are you doing out here, trying to catch pneumonia?"

"I could ask you the same thing," I said.

"Don't tell me that O.P. has had too much to drink again," he said.

"Not only that but he's disappeared with Melissa," I said, discovering as I said it that I didn't care at all. As far as I was concerned, she could carry him off and never bring him back.

"Don't worry," Charles said. "He'll soon pass out. He always does." There was a pause. I was conscious of his looking at me. "Hey, you're shivering," he said.

"I don't think cotton jeans and short sleeves were made for this climate," I said.

"You want to come and share my swing? It's pretty cozy, here, and it'll be even cozier with two."

I sat beside him. "You're right. It is cozy."

For a while we rocked in silence.

"You know, I think I misjudged you," Charles said at last. "I thought you weren't at all like Stephanie. Now I think I was wrong. You are like her in some ways after all."

"In what ways?"

"I don't know. I thought you were—how you looked—you know, hard as nails, cool, and calm. But I can see now that you're sensitive like she is, only you hide it better. How is she, by the way?"

"Oh, fine, I guess."

Another pause.

"Do you call her often?"

"Not too often." This was ridiculous. Why did I have to go on pretending to him? It was so comforting to feel him warm and close beside me. I longed to snuggle my head on his shoulder and just forget all this stupid business, but how could I?

"I miss her," he said at last. "I only knew her for such a short time, but as soon as we started talking, I knew I had found someone who was on my wavelength. I've even forgiven her for lying to me. I've been doing a lot of thinking, and I can understand why she was jealous of you. After all, her voice is just as good as yours, and yet she's gotten nowhere, and you've got everything you want. I'd be jealous, too."

We sat in silence. We could hear the noises coming out from the party, as if from very far away. Above our heads the swing squeaked rhythmically as we rocked back and forth. I kept opening my mouth to say, "But I really am Stephanie." But each time I thought of all those

132

people at the party, of O.P. and his temper, and above all, of Charles, who had just forgiven me for deceiving him the first time.

"Would you do me a favor?" I asked. "Would you drive me home?"

We drove home in silence. Our breath rose like clouds of smoke in the cold car. As we pulled up outside my grandmother's house, Charles touched my hand. "You're a nice girl, Stormy," he said. "But you can't ever replace your sister. Would you ask her to come back real soon?"

I ran into the house. Grandma had fallen asleep watching an old Ingrid Bergman movie on TV. I crept past her up the stairs.

Charles misses me, Charles wants me back, I thought happily, then suddenly I remembered something that stood in the way of getting rid of Stormy—something that stood in the way of everything. I had promised a whole roomful of kids that I would bring a famous rock star to their school.

Now what have you done? I said to myself. *How are you ever going to get out of this one?*

Chapter Sixteen

My eyes were burning, and my brain was wide awake.

How can you be so dumb? I asked myself over and over again as I tossed and turned, trying desperately to sleep. *What made me do it? Why did I have to go and say I knew Billy Case? Now I'll just have to go to school in the morning and tell them that the whole thing was a fraud and I don't know anybody, and everyone will hate me.*

I wriggled uncomfortably in bed, trying to pull the covers over my head and blot out a world that had suddenly become too complicated.

It's not as if I were like Carly, I thought. *I bet Carly would know all about Billy Case. She'd probably just go down to the theater he was playing in and say, "How about coming to sing for us." She'd probably even—*

I stopped short and sat upright in bed. Carly knew everything about rock stars, and Billy Case

134

was one of her favorites. She'd know where he was performing. I bet she'd even know a way to get in and see him. If only I could come face to face with him and confess how dumb I had been, maybe, just maybe, he'd have pity on me and come to our school.

The clock on the stand beside my bed said 2:00 A.M. I was dying to call Carly, but I didn't think she'd be in her best mood if I woke her then. Her parents wouldn't be too amused, either. I suppose I must have dozed on and off, but I kept waking up and watching the hands of the clock creep around slowly. At six-thirty I couldn't wait a minute longer. I crept downstairs and called her.

"Wassamatter?" she mumbled after her father had yelled for her to wake up.

"Sorry to wake you, Carly, but it's a real emergency," I said.

"It had better be," she growled. "You know how much I treasure that last half hour of sleep. That's when I always have the best dreams. You have no idea what you just called me away from."

"Don't tell me now," I pleaded. "Are you awake enough to listen?"

"I'm awake. So what's the emergency?"

"I've got to talk to you about Billy Case."

"You what?"

"I have to talk about Billy Case. You know, the rock star. The one you kept kissing the last time I visited."

"Billy Case is an emergency?" she asked. "I'm off him, actually. Now it's Joe Elliot who's tops."

"I don't need Joe Elliot—I need your help."

"To do what?"

"To meet Billy Case."

"You woke me up to tell me you want to meet Billy Case?" she yelled, almost blasting the phone away from my ear. "Have you flipped? Let me tell you that you can't even get near any star at a concert. They have security men all around them, and all you ever get to see is a glimpse of their behinds as they climb into their limos. Even I, greatest rock fan in all of New York, have never actually met a rock star. Not face to face, that is."

"But you know all about them—where they live and what they wear and everything. Surely you could get me to meet him if it really mattered."

"I could take you where you'd catch a glimpse of him," she said hesitantly.

"That's not good enough. I've got to talk to him."

"No way. Don't you think every girl in the world wants to talk to him? He's almost an international star these days. Maybe last year you could have met him, before he toured with Pink Floyd. What do you want to tell him, anyway? Are you hooked on Billy Case?"

"I have to invite him to come and sing at our school."

"Ha, ha. Very funny."

We had to pause a few minutes while Carly went into hysterics on the other end of the phone.

"Do you realize," she spluttered at last, "how many people ask rock stars to come and sing for them? What on earth makes you think he would listen to you? Just forget it. Go back to bed."

"But you don't understand, Carly. I told the kids that I knew, that Stormy knew, Billy Case, and I promised to get him for our big fund raiser because he was born in Hartford."

"What on earth made you do a dumb thing like that?" she asked.

"Don't rub it in." I sighed. "I know it was dumb. I sort of got trapped into it."

"So just tell them that he can't come. Tell them he's in Europe now."

"I guess that's what I'll have to do," I said. "But it's sort of a challenge. You know they want some proof that I'm really a rock star. I guess they're getting sick of all my talk and no action."

There was a pause and heavy breathing from Carly's end. "I don't really see how . . ." she said at last. "Are you sure you don't want to go for Joe Elliot—I know more about him right now. He's touring in Australia."

"Great. I'll just fly down and bring back a few kangaroos as well," I said. "It's OK. I'll admit defeat. It was just a long shot that you could help. Expect to see a crushed failure crawling home shortly. After we worked so hard on my new identity. And it worked so well, up until now that is."

"I'll tell you what," Carly said. "Give me today, and I'll ask around about Billy Case. At least I can find out where he's performing right now. He might be on the West Coast for all I know."

"Thanks, Carly," I said. "You're a true friend."

The day at school was terrible—almost unbearable. As usual the news had spread all through the school, and kids kept coming up to me and saying things like, "You're terrific. I hear you're getting Billy Case for us."

When one kid in a wheelchair said, "I know they'll get enough money for that elevator now," I felt so bad I almost confessed right then and there. But I managed to keep going until the end of the day.

"Your friend Carly called you," Grandma said as soon as I got in. "She says it's urgent."

I rushed across the room and began dialing furiously.

"Listen to this!" Carly yelled as soon as she picked up the phone. "He's got a concert here tomorrow night. He'll actually be in New York City. Isn't that luck?"

"Great," I said flatly. "Now I, in company with three million other girls, have a good chance of meeting him. Maybe I could throw myself in front of his car. I wish I could change myself into a fly on his dressing room wall."

Slowly an idea began to form in my mind.

"Hey, Steph, are you still there?" Carly asked.

"I'm thinking, shut up a minute."

"Well, I wouldn't want to interrupt such a rare occurrence as your thinking," Carly said stiffly.

"Carly," I said at last, "how about if we disguise ourselves as something and sneak into his dressing room and wait until he comes—"

"There are a couple of things wrong with that,"

she said. "First, I don't like the way you said *we*. You weren't, by any chance, including me in this scheme, were you? Because, let me tell you right now, I have no desire to be thrown out of a theater by large security men."

"But, Carly, you've been such a help to me in everything. Don't you want to see it through to the end?"

"Not if the end is going to be a total disaster, thank you, no. There are limits to friendship that I can't meet, Stephanie Fenton," she said. "I've bleached your hair, lent you half my clothes, and turned you into an instant success. But now is not a good time to get on the wrong side of my parents. I'm already in their bad book for staying out late a couple of times. If I land in jail, I don't think they'd be too understanding."

"We won't end up in jail," I pleaded. "The worst thing that can happen to us, the very worst, is that they throw us out. And I don't really mean 'throw.' I mean escort us out."

" 'Throw' is probably more accurate, and I bruise easily," she muttered.

"Come on, Carly," I begged. "You're the expert on rock stars. I wouldn't be able to find my way into a dressing room without you, and if we were disguised properly—"

"What do you plan on disguising yourself as—a can of Pepsi or a doughnut? That's what Billy Case likes, by the way, Pepsi and chocolate doughnuts."

"Then that's fantastic!" I shouted.

"You really are going to disguise yourself as a chocolate doughnut?"

"No, dummy. We'll say that we're from the doughnut shop, and we're delivering doughnuts to him."

"And the doorman will certainly buy that," Carly said sarcastically. "He'll think it's very normal that a doughnut shop would send over two teenage girls with one order."

"Well, we could try it," I said. "It's better than hiding in garbage cans or climbing in through the heating vents. And I promise, Carly, if we get into trouble, I'll tell them it was all my idea and I forced you into it. Please, Carly, please say you'll do it with me. I'm too scared to do it on my own."

"One of these days I'm going to regret I ever met you," she said, then paused. "OK," she said at last, giving a long sigh. "I'll come with you. Though personally I think it's the most stupid, most idiotic thing I have done in my entire life."

Chapter Seventeen

The train to New York seemed to take forever. It was too hot, and I still hadn't recovered from my sleepless night. I kept dozing fitfully, having horrible nightmares about huge security guards who threw me into garbage cans, and then I'd wake up with a start. I wished I could wake up to find that the entire thing was a dream—that there had never been any Stormy Fenton. I wished my stomach wouldn't feel as though it were being run over by the train. I wished my mind wouldn't keep running through all the things that could go wrong.

I had sneaked out early without waking Grandma, leaving her a scrawled note saying that I was out for the day with O.P. I hated lying to her, but I had a suspicion that she would have forbidden me to go if she had known where I was going. I knew she would have forbidden me if she had found out what I intended to do when I got there. My parents had heard about my last trip to New York, and they weren't very pleased. Mom had a fit over the phone, wondering what kind of grandmother would let a granddaughter run around the country unsupervised.

What was I turning into? A girl who lied to her grandmother, that's what! And lied to a grandmother who was one of the most understanding adults in the world.

"Well, the doughnut plan wasn't such a good idea," I said to Carly in the cab on the way to the theater. "We don't have uniforms or anything. They probably wouldn't even believe we came from a doughnut store. But I thought of something else on the train. I think I could pull it off—maybe."

Carly listened patiently while I filled her in on my new scheme. She was quiet after I finally finished.

"I have to watch you make a complete fool of yourself during this drama," Carly said slowly. Then she sighed. "If worse comes to worst, I can always say I'm your escort back to the funny farm!"

"Most amusing," I said. "I don't think you have any faith in my acting ability."

By then we had arrived at the theater, and my own faith in myself started to evaporate. The theater was large and impressive looking. "I'm almost tempted to go back for those doughnuts," I whispered to Carly.

She looked at me seriously and nodded. "Good idea," she said. "And I'm almost tempted to wait for you at the police station."

"Fine," I said. "Turn down a chance to meet Billy Case and get his autograph in his dressing room."

"Oh, OK," she said with a big sigh. "I know I need my head examined, but I'll also need your help with my math homework next year. Not that we'll have any brains left once the security guard is through with us."

The stage door was down a side alley, which was dark, dingy, and smelled of garbage. As we walked quietly down the alley, I started to really lose my nerve. "I think I'll just forget about it after all," I whispered, clutching Carly's arm. "I'll just go to school, confess, and let everyone hate me for the rest of my life."

"You are not chickening out now that we've come this far," Carly said. "I don't want to have gotten up on a Saturday for nothing. Now remember, you are Stormy Fenton, famous rock star, and get in there."

My plan depended entirely on my acting ability. I figured that I had so much experience with my role as Stormy that I would do best to stick with it rather than try a new one like the doughnut-delivery girl. I was going to convince everyone—from the doorman to Billy Case himself—that I was the hit-maker Stormy Fenton and that they had met me thousands of times before. I would rush up to Billy, all sweet and slobbery, and hug him and coo, "Oh, Billy, I've missed you so badly. But before I forget, Mick sends his greetings." He would be too embarrassed to admit that he had never seen this weirdo before.

The scene had gone smoothly as I mapped it out on the train, but now, as Carly was pushing me through the heavy door, I went flying in a lot quicker than I had planned. I had only just regained my balance when I found myself eyeball to eyeball with an old man, scowling at me from behind a desk.

"This is the stage door," he growled. "Private. No admittance. Can't you read?"

This is it, Stormy Fenton, I thought. *You always thought you should be a star. Now's your big chance to prove it, so don't blow it.* I took a deep breath.

"Is Mr. Case in the theater yet?"

"He's in the theater, and he doesn't want no little teenagers hanging around him, either. Now beat it before I call the cops," he growled.

Stormy Fenton smiled and ran a hand through her short, blond curls. "I guess you don't do too many rock concerts in this theater," she said in her most starlike voice, "or you'd recognize me. Would you be a honey and run upstairs and tell Billy that Stormy just flew in from England and has to say hi. I didn't even say goodbye to him after that party, and I felt so bad. I only have a few minutes before my plane leaves for L.A. So please hurry, there's a sweetie pie."

The old man scowled at me, but not in the same way he had before. "I'm not allowed to leave this desk," he said.

"But Billy will be furious with you if he finds he's missed me," I said sweetly.

"If you want to see him, you'd best go up

yourself," he snapped. "Up one flight, third door on the right."

I was already on the first stair when I heard his voice again, "Hey, where do you think you're going?" he yelled. "Is she with you, miss?"

I turned back to Carly, who looked like she was about to faint. "Oh, she's my hairdresser," I said. "I never travel without her."

As soon as we had turned the first corner, we exploded into giggles.

"Your hairdresser! Are you crazy?" Carly whispered.

"I had to get you in somehow, and that was the first thing that came into my head," I whispered back. "Now follow me and look like a hairdresser."

I didn't allow myself time to think before I knocked loudly on Billy Case's door. As soon as it was opened, I swept in. I had reached that stage of my suicide mission when they would have to put me in chains to stop me.

"Billy darling," I purred before he could speak. "I felt so bad that I left without saying goodbye." I swept over and kissed the tall young man on the cheek. "It was a terrific party, don't you think?" I babbled on. "The best one I went to in London."

I could feel Carly kicking me, nudging me in the back, but I didn't stop. "And I really didn't want to leave, but I had to catch the Concorde, and you know what a drag it is to fly any other way. So I decided I had to see you again for a few minutes before I went on to L.A.—"

I stopped and paused for breath. Everything

145

was going just as I had planned. Carly had stopped kicking me, too. The young man looked down at me coldly. "Is this some sort of stunt?" he asked. "The newspapers put you up to this?"

"What do you mean?" I asked angrily. "Don't you remember that party? I know you were pretty drunk, but surely you must remember the good time we had, Billy."

"I would have remembered it if I'd been there," he said calmly. "There's just one small detail you've got wrong. I'm not Billy."

Suddenly I wasn't Stormy anymore. I was plain old Stephanie, with flaming cheeks and the blood singing in my ears.

"You're—you're not?" I stammered.

"No, I'm not. I'm his manager."

"That's what I was trying to tell you," Carly hissed into the back of my neck. "But you wouldn't pay any attention."

"Oh, I'm sorry," I said. "I feel so stupid. I just had to get in to see Billy and now—" Before I could stop them, two tears trickled down my cheeks, cutting lines through my makeup.

The manager's face softened a little. "It's OK. Girls try to get in here all the time. You did better than most of them. Most of them don't make it past the doorman. You just go quickly and quietly, and I'll get Billy to send you an autographed picture, OK?"

"Just a minute, Barry," came a voice from an inner room. "I want to get a look at the girl I was supposed to have spent such a wild night with."

Then Billy Case himself came through the

door. Of course, I recognized him from Carly's pictures the minute I saw him and wondered how I could have been so dumb. I stood there, wishing the floor would open up and swallow me while Billy Case eyed me closely, grinning all the time.

"Nah," he said. "Not my type at all. I like the feminine type—long curls and frilly dresses. Nice try, though. You want my autograph?"

"I didn't do all this just for an autograph," I said. "I promised the kids at school that I'd get you to come and sing for the elevator fund."

"The what?"

"They want to put in an elevator for the handicapped kids," I said. "And we need to raise a lot of money fast."

"I see," he said. "People ask me all the time to do personal appearances. If I sang everywhere for nothing, I wouldn't eat."

"But we thought this one might be special," I said, "because we knew you grew up in Hartford."

"You're from Hartford High?"

"Close to it—Weybridge High."

"Weybridge High!" he said and laughed. "We used to beat you guys at football all the time."

"The football team's not too good," I admitted. "But we're such a small school."

Billy walked across the room and perched on the edge of his dressing table. "What I don't understand," he said, "is why you tried to pull this dumb stunt on me. If you'd only written a letter, I might have come. A stunt like this would only annoy me."

"You'd never have gotten the letter," I said. "Your manager would have thrown it into the nearest trash can. And I *know* the stunt was dumb now. Only I had to try and use it because the kids were counting on me. I had already pulled one dumb stunt at school, you see. I told the kids I was a rock star and that I knew you."

"What?" He almost burst out laughing. "What made you do that?"

I had come this far, and I figured I had nothing to lose by telling the truth. I shrugged my shoulders. "I guess I wanted to be noticed by the most popular kids. I told everyone I was a big rock star in England," I said. "I sort of got trapped into admitting I knew you. I'm sorry. I feel so stupid now."

Billy gave me a smile. "Well, you've got guts, I'll say that for you. I tell you what—I won't promise anything, but if you guys can arrange a concert before I leave on tour in two weeks, I'll see if I can come. It would be sort of fun to go home again, and old Weybridge High needs all the help it can get."

"You'd really do that?" I asked. "I don't know how to thank you!"

"I guess it's because I'm basically a wonderful person," he said and smiled at himself in the mirror.

"And modest, too," his manager added. "Now, will you girls get out of here? Here, take my card. You can phone me about the details. Don't you bother Billy again. He should be on stage right now rehearsing."

"Thanks," I said, taking the card. We walked toward the door.

"Hey, kid," Billy Case called after me. I turned to look back at him, still perched on the edge of the table looking relaxed and amused. "Now you do know Billy Case, right?" And he gave me a wink.

Chapter Eighteen

The news that Billy Case was coming put the whole school into a frenzy. It should have been my big moment—the thing I could have told my grandchildren about one day: "And did I ever tell you about the time I went to New York and persuaded a famous rock star to sing at our school?" Not only that, but the committee who was planning the concert had asked O.P.'s group to play and me to sing an opening number as a warm-up for Billy. What a great opportunity. Not only had I managed to "prove" that I was Stormy, but here was my chance at fame and fortune. It was what I had always dreamed of—proving to the world and myself that I could make it.

But somehow it had gotten twisted along the way. I was no longer sure I wanted to be a rock star. I was glad to have had my chance at the glamour, glad to have been able to sing in public, and glad to have had people tell me I was good, but now I felt inclined to quit.

"I've decided that I'm not really destined to be a rock star," I told my grandmother as I was getting ready for the big concert on Friday night.

"Of course not, you're much too sensitive," my grandmother agreed. "And much too sensible, too. What a horrible life—living in hotel rooms and always on a bus or a plane, not to mention the drugs and the drink. And think of how many people actually make it to the top! Most kids go through all the struggle, the tryouts, and the cheap hotels and never see their names up in lights. If you ask me, I think it has to be in your blood from birth, and I can tell you definitely that it's not in yours."

I laughed and finished putting on my makeup.

"How are you getting to school?" she asked. "Do you need a ride?"

"O.P.'s coming to pick me up."

"O.P.?" She raised an eyebrow. "I thought that was all over and forgotten."

"He suddenly decided to be interested in me again when he found out I was bringing Billy Case to school," I said. "But I'm not fooled this time. I'm using him for rides to school just as much as he's using me. I've wised up about people like O.P."

"Well, you've certainly grown up a lot in a short time," Grandma said. "I think your experiment with a new image has been a success. It's made you think more about what people are really like underneath all the glitter."

"But I just wish—" I said and then hesitated.

"You wish what?"

"Nothing." I picked up my purse. I wanted to

tell her I wished I had let Charles share my secret, and Laurie, too; and that I had known at the beginning what I knew now about what was real and what wasn't. Still, it was too late to undo any of my dumb deeds. I would live out my remaining time as Stormy, then I would go back to being Stephanie, and probably someday I would forget that I ever knew a great guy called Charles. . . .

"Hey, you look terrific," O.P. said, putting an arm around me as I got into his car. "I bet Billy Case asks you to go on tour with him."

"I'm not his type," I said. "He told me once. He likes romantic girls with long hair and frills."

"I mean as a singer," O.P. said. "When he hears you sing, he'll have to sign you up or something—and then you'll need a good back-up group, won't you?"

"And I wonder who that would be?" I asked with a smile. It felt good to have the upper hand with O.P. He no longer had any power to hurt or to impress me. I could see through everything he said; he was as easy to read as a comic book.

"I'm going to do 'It's All Over Now' with the group tonight," O.P. said, staring ahead into the darkness as he drove. "That has a drum solo in it."

"Good luck," I said. "I hope you make it." The funny thing was that I really meant it. He couldn't help the way he was any more than I could. He wanted to succeed so very badly.

The school auditorium looked strangely elegant with spotlights on its blue velvet curtain. I realized for the first time that I was going to have to get up on that stage and sing in front of an audience full of people who thought I was an experienced performer. The school dance had been one thing; after all, everybody goes to dances to have a good time—they don't really care what the singing is like. I had a sudden, acute attack of butterflies. I sat down just inside the curtain and clutched my knees to my chest, rocking back and forth to calm myself. While I was sitting there, I heard footsteps on the other side of the curtain. They came closer, then stopped.

"And don't let Stormy know, for heaven's sakes," I heard someone mutter. It was O.P.

"She'll kill you afterward," Gary commented.

"Who cares about afterward. Afterward I'll be signed up with a good manager. I'll have a great song to record."

"OK. You're the boss," Gary said. I could hear the doubt in his voice. "Are you going to tell Billy Case you wrote the song yourself?"

"Why not? It's not copyrighted or anything. I'll announce it as a surprise after she walks offstage. I'll say it's just a little thing I wrote that expresses how I really feel—or something like that—"

"But you don't even know all the words. She never sang you the whole thing."

"So? I've written some of my own to fill in the gaps. It'll be good enough, believe me. It's a terrific song—a real hit."

"You'd better get down and tell Pete about it," Gary said. "You know he doesn't like surprises."

"I was hoping you'd do that, Gary, old buddy," O.P. said. "You know him better than me."

"Coward."

"Not at all. I've got to comb my hair before we go onstage."

I heard O.P. laughing as he walked away. I sat there unable to move. The butterflies had all flown, quickly replaced by anger. So O.P. was going to sing Charles's song and claim it was his own. He was going to sneak it in behind my back. How could he do such a dirty trick? And what would Charles think of me? I remembered how hurt Charles said he was when his old girlfriend Becky had sung one of his songs in public. Now he'd think I'd given the song to O.P., or rather Stephanie had given the song to Stormy, and I'd passed it along to O.P. That looked doubly bad, as if both of the Fenton twins were rats. Somehow I had to stop O.P. I was scared of his temper, but I wasn't going to let Charles get hurt again.

I followed O.P. toward his dressing room. Actually, dressing room was a fancy name for a supply closet with a mirror. We only had two real dressing rooms, and, of course, Billy and his group got those. I had to make do with the girls' bathroom.

O.P. was alone in the supply closet, running a comb through his hair and patting it in place. I went up behind him and tapped him on the shoulder.

"Hi, honey," he said sweetly, smiling at me in the mirror.

"You and I have to talk," I said coldly. "I was sitting behind the stage curtain just now. I heard everything you said about singing that song. You are one of the lowest, slimiest, creepiest people I have ever met. If you go onstage and sing that song, I'll announce to the whole world that you stole it. Then Billy Case won't look at you twice, even if you were the greatest drummer in the world, which you're not!"

He was quiet for a minute, surprised at having been caught. Finally he said meekly, "If that's how you feel I guess I won't do it then. Fine. You win. Here, hand me my tux, will you?"

I was dazed by my easy victory. I reached around to get his tux, but it wasn't there. Nothing was there but a rapid movement behind me, followed by the sound of the door shutting and the key turning in the lock.

I rushed to the door. "O.P. let me out of here," I yelled angrily.

"Sorry, honey. I don't quit that easily," came his calm, smooth voice. "I'm real sorry to have to do this to you, but you are not going to blow my big chance. I'll let you out after the concert is over. By the way, I have my tux—don't worry."

"Don't you think they might miss me?" I asked, trying to play the rock star again.

"I'll make an announcement that you suddenly got sick."

Then I could only hear his footsteps echoing down the hall as he walked away. I stood by the door, torn between anger and fear. I was terrified of being in small spaces, and the supply closet certainly qualified as one. I grabbed the door and rattled it fiercely. I pounded on it and yelled. Nobody came. There was no one to come. O.P.'s group would have been onstage already, and no one else would have any reason to come down that hallway. I thought about movies where heroes put their fists or feet through doors— surely the school janitor would understand if I broke down his door. I tried a couple of kicks but only succeeded in bruising my toes. It was not the sort of door a normal person could break down. It was solid wood, and unless Superman happened to be in the neighborhood, I was trapped.

All my fighting energy drained out of me at that point. I was scared and alone. I knew I wasn't in any danger, but that small, stuffy room, with its one naked light bulb glaring at me from the ceiling, made me panic. I found I was gasping for breath.

"This is stupid," I said, trying to control myself. "You have nothing to be scared of. At the very worst you'll miss a concert and O.P. will sing Charles's song. Big deal! The world is not coming to an end." The pep talk helped me a little, and I started to pace up and down. Then I noticed something that O.P. hadn't. There was a small window, high on the wall. It was probably too small to crawl through and probably locked, but the sight of it gave me hope.

I dragged a rickety chair over to it and climbed up. The window was bigger than I had thought, but the catch was jammed solid. The window had obviously never been opened during this century. The only other thing to do was break the glass, which was worth a chance. Even if I couldn't fit through, maybe someone would hear the sound of glass breaking and come help. Anything to get out of there!

I took off my shoe and hit the glass. In movies and books it's never mentioned how hard you have to hit a piece of glass to break it. I whacked my shoe on it several times, and all I got was a slightly bent shoe. I looked around for something else to use and found a wooden coat hanger. The glass shattered in a shower of flying pieces. What was left of the window was a horrible jagged edge that no one in his or her right mind would want to climb through. Standing on the chair, I peered out and yelled for help. Of course, the window would be facing the rear of the building and the football field. Who would be likely to be on the football field at that time of night?

"Somehow you are going to have to crawl through that," I told myself. But I wasn't very anxious to start. I didn't think I'd look good onstage with my clothes, and possibly skin, too, cut to ribbons. I whacked away at the glass and got most of the pieces out. But I still needed something to pad the edges. I had no hesitation using O.P.'s sweater and jacket for the job. It took me a few minutes of wriggling and struggling to get through the window. Finally I fell to the ground outside in a heap.

I must have looked a mess. I could see I had scratched my bare arms and gotten dust all over my black jeans. I had probably smudged my makeup and ruined my blouse as well. Having lost one shoe on the closet floor, I limped to the front of the building.

"Ticket, please," the girl at the entrance said, barring my way.

"Don't be dumb; I'm a performer," I snapped. "I got locked out by mistake. I should be onstage right now!" Then, not waiting to argue anymore, I pushed her out of my way.

O.P. was standing at the microphone. "And we're very sorry to say that she was suddenly taken ill right before the performance," he was saying. "She sends her love and wishes she could be here with us tonight." Billy Case and his group were sitting at one side of the stage in positions of honor. The other members of O.P.'s group were standing with their instruments and had probably just finished a number.

I took a deep breath and ran down the aisle. "Relax, everyone," I shouted, jumping up onto the stage. "It wasn't anything serious after all. I've made a spectacular recovery and have come straight from the hospital to be with you."

The audience broke into loud applause. I took the microphone from O.P. before he could even close his mouth. "Thank you so much," I said. "Now, if I could borrow a guitar from someone. . . ." I adjusted the microphone stand and replaced the mike, before leaning over and taking Gary's guitar. "I'd like to play you a surprise song. This song was written by someone in this school, and frankly, it's the best song I've ever heard. I'd like Billy Case to have the chance to hear it and know who wrote it."

I strummed the guitar and started to sing. The crowd was totally silent. My voice and the one guitar sounded very small. I hesitated over the first few phrases, but then as my confidence grew, the music grew. I pounded out the chorus.

Suddenly I was aware of an interruption. Someone was running up the center aisle toward me. He leaped onto the stage and snatched the guitar from me.

"That is my song," Charles shouted angrily, "and I did not give you or anyone else permission to sing it." He turned to the audience. "I'm sorry, everyone, but this song is personal. I never intended to have it performed in public." He turned to look at me, and there was a wild and desperate expression on his face. "You and your sister, you're both bad news," he said. Then he turned his back on me and started offstage. I grabbed wildly at his shirt-sleeve, not thinking about how stupid I looked, only knowing that I couldn't let Charles go like that. It had to be then or never. . . .

"Charles, wait, I can explain," I called. My voice was amplified all over the auditorium, but I had forgotten all the people who were sitting below me. I had forgotten that I should have been performing.

"O.P. heard me singing your song. I didn't mean him to, but he really liked it, and he was going to sing it tonight for Billy Case and claim that it was his own. I tried to stop him, I really did, but he locked me in a supply closet. That's why he was telling the audience I was sick. I had to smash a window to climb out—see?" The words came tumbling out. When I finally paused for breath, I held up my scratched arms, hoping he would understand.

Instead he looked at me coldly. "If your sister Stephanie hadn't broken her promise to me in the first place, you'd never have heard my song at all," he said. "I don't trust you or your sister."

The whole auditorium had fallen deathly quiet. Charles's voice had rung out from the stage, and I became painfully conscious of all the people staring up at me and waiting. I took a deep breath. "Stephanie wouldn't break a promise to you, Charles," I told him. "She wouldn't do anything to hurt you—because she really cares about you."

"What do you know about anything?" Charles asked coldly.

"I know because I *am* Stephanie," I said. "I never was Stormy. I'm only Stephanie with a new haircut. Stormy doesn't exist."

There was a moment's total silence, then a great commotion began in the audience. I could hear a few shouts and giggles, but mostly gasps of pure astonishment.

"I don't believe this," came O.P.'s angry voice from behind me. "How could you do a thing like that to me?"

Charles's eyes met mine. He looked confused, hurt, and still very, very angry. "I don't know what to believe anymore," he said, "and what's more I don't want to know."

Then he turned and ran offstage, disappearing into the darkness behind the curtains.

"Charles, please wait," I called. I pushed past the musicians onstage and rushed out after him. I could hear the excited buzz of the audience and then the sounds of the band trying to regain control. But I didn't care what was happening onstage. I didn't even care that I had gotten even with O.P. I just knew that I had to catch Charles and make everything all right. As I ran out into the school yard, I heard a car rev up and drive away, tires screeching.

Chapter Nineteen

I don't remember getting home. I suppose I walked or ran all the way because the tears that had flowed down my cheeks were frozen into miniature icicles. I didn't really come to properly until I was sitting in Grandma's living room, sipping peppermint tea and unthawing. "Grandma, what am I going to do?" I asked with a big sigh. As I unthawed and sipped, I tried to explain the whole thing to her, starting with the first day at school right up to the scene with O.P. that night.

"It seems so unfair. I was only singing the stupid song to stop O.P. from singing it and claiming it was his. I was planning to announce Charles's name at the end, then everybody would have told him how great it was. Now he'll never forgive me."

Grandma stared thoughtfully into the fire. "All in all, you've made quite a mess of things, haven't you?" she said. "What a nonsensical idea—to pretend you were your own sister! Don't you know that you can never escape from yourself and it was only you who let yourself down?"

"What do you mean?" I asked.

Grandma looked up. Her steel blue eyes met mine. "I know it's not easy being an only child," she said. "You are brought up to think that you are the center of the universe and that the earth, sun, and stars all revolve around you."

"I do not think that," I said angrily. "If anything, it's the opposite. I feel that nobody notices me, or at least, I did feel that way until I changed into Stormy."

"You might have felt that way," she said, smiling at me kindly, "but you still acted as if you were the only person alive. Did you consider anyone else's feelings? Did you consider that you might hurt Laurie or Charles by not telling them your plans? Did you ever stop to consider whether Carly really wanted to go along with your schemes? I don't think so."

"I thought about Charles's feelings," I said. "I climbed through a broken window and made a fool of myself just to protect him."

"But you sang his song when you promised not to."

"Only to stop O.P. from singing it."

"You could have done what Charles did—prevent it from being sung at all," Grandma said slowly. "I think that secretly you wanted that Billy person to hear how well you performed a good song."

"Yes, I wanted Billy to hear it," I said, "but

not for me—for Charles. I wanted Billy to like his song."

"Even though Charles made it quite clear he didn't want it sung in public?"

"He didn't know what a good song it was," I argued. "I thought he'd be pleased when everyone liked it."

"So, there you are," Grandma said. "You do think you know better than other people. You try to manage their lives. You've got to learn that that's not the way to make friends and keep them, Stephanie."

"OK, but what do I do now?"

Grandma sighed. "Learn from your mistakes, I guess."

"But I want Charles to forgive me—"

"I'd leave that alone, honey. There's not much you can do now, and it's really not such a big thing—"

"It is to me," I cried. "Grandma, I really care about Charles. I didn't mean to hurt him. I'd do anything to make things right."

"In that case, good luck," she said. "What do you intend to do?"

"I wish I knew," I said miserably. "Right now I think I'll just go to bed."

I didn't sleep well, and in the morning nothing seemed any more hopeful than it had the night before. After breakfast Grandma went out jogging. I sat alone, waiting for the telephone to ring. Surely Charles would have thought about things and have decided to forgive me—surely that phone would ring any minute, and he'd tell me that he cared about me, too. But it didn't. By midafternoon my grandmother got annoyed with me.

"For heaven's sake stop sitting there like a statue," she said. "It's a nice, clear afternoon. Go out and get some fresh air, you'll feel much better."

I didn't honestly believe that anything, except a phone call from Charles, would make me feel better, but I went out anyway. It was a glorious day, one of those sparkling winter afternoons when the sky looks as if it's cut from blue glass, but I stamped along, kicking savagely at stones and twigs and not noticing anything that I passed. I told myself I was just wandering aimlessly through town, but I soon was heading straight for Charles's house. I walked past it three times. I kept hoping for a miracle—that he would see me from a window and come running down. But he didn't. There was no sign of life behind those heavy drapes, and I couldn't find the courage to knock on the door.

Just admit that it's all over between you and Charles, I told myself. *After all, he isn't the only boy in a great big world. There will be others.*

But I don't want others, I thought miserably. I turned the corner, and the house vanished from sight.

I didn't notice the figure coming down the sidewalk toward me until I got entangled in a dog's leash and almost tripped.

"Hey, watch where you're going," said a familiar voice. I looked up and saw it was Laurie. We stared at each other uneasily for a moment. I sensed that she was about to walk away again and desperately tried to think of the right thing, or anything, to say to her.

"Look, Laurie—" I began hesitantly.

"Are you really Stephanie?" she asked at the same time.

I nodded.

"Cross your heart and hope to die?"

"Cross my heart and hope to die."

She kept on looking at me. "So how come you didn't tell me?" she asked angrily.

"I wanted to tell you, Laurie," I said. "That first night when I came to your front door, I just wanted to try out my disguise on you, to see if I could fool you. I was planning to let you in on the secret, but your sister showed up at the door, and you wouldn't speak to me after that."

"I know," she said. "I was mad. What a lot of time we've wasted, haven't we? All the while I kept wishing Stephanie would come back, and you were here all the time. If only I'd known!"

"We could have had a lot of fun," I said. "I should have made you listen."

"I probably wouldn't have," Laurie said. "I can be kind of stubborn."

Without warning she grabbed me and started shaking me. "You fooled me all this time, you creep!" she yelled. "And what a fantastic thing to do! You got O.P. for a boyfriend, and you brought Billy Case to our school. And now all the kids know that you're a terrific actress, also. I can't get over it!" She started laughing, and we both laughed and hugged each other and laughed some more.

"But what happens now?" she asked. "Will you go on dating O.P.?"

"No way! I'd rather shave my head than date that guy," I said. "Let me tell you something, Laurie. The only thing that gorgeous guys think about is themselves. Give me an ordinary sort of guy any day."

"Do I take that to mean that you and Charles—?"

"I wish," I said. "But I don't know how to get him back, Laurie. I don't think he'll ever trust me again."

"He's been really hurt, Steph," Laurie said. "Ever since he thought Stephanie left without saying goodbye, he's been hurting. You'll just have to give him more time."

"But I don't have that much more time," I said and sighed. "I couldn't bear it if I had to leave with the memory of him hating me. I really love him, Laurie. I said he was ordinary, but he's not ordinary at all. In fact he's very special. Have you ever noticed that cute little smile of his, just like Christopher Reeve in *Superman*, and the wonderful songs he writes and—"

"You don't have to go on," Laurie said, grinning. "I get the picture. I know true love when I see it. I hope it all works out for you. He's a nice boy. Not like that nerd Gary I've been worshipping all this time."

"What happened?"

"Nothing. That's the trouble. He still doesn't notice I exist. I mean, any boy who can ignore a cute girl like me for that long can't be worth much, can he? So I'm through with him. Besides, I met this guy jogging in the park—"

"You were jogging in the park?"

"Not me. Him. I was standing there, and he cut through the bushes. You meet a lot of interesting people that way."

We both started to laugh again. Laurie walked me to my house, her dog leading the way, and we laughed all the way home. It was really good to have a friend beside me again, and I felt almost hopeful that somehow I could win back Charles. . . .

Chapter Twenty

Laurie accompanied me to school Monday morning. I was very glad to have her beside me because, to tell the truth, I was scared of facing all those kids again. What would they think of me now? Would they be mad that I had deceived them, that I had claimed to be someone I wasn't?

I felt all those eyes examining me as we crossed the school yard.

"You wanted to be noticed," Laurie said. "And you've certainly made everyone notice you. I bet there isn't a kid in the school who doesn't know all about you."

"I sure hope they're going to be understanding about it," I worried.

"Why wouldn't they be?" Laurie asked. "After all, you did manage to bring Billy Case to school and made a lot of money for the elevator fund."

We walked up the steps. A couple turned toward us.

"Hey, Stormy, or is it Stephanie?" the boy called.

"Stephanie," I said, feeling myself blushing. "Just plain old Stephanie again."

"That was a great stunt, Stephanie," he said. "You sure had us fooled." They moved toward us.

"So it is true that you aren't a real rock star?" the girl asked.

"I'm afraid so," I said. "I'm just a regular kid."

"You have some nerve," the girl said. "And we all thought you were somebody."

"Cut it out, Linda—she did bring Billy Case, didn't she?" the boy said.

"I bet someone else got him to come here, and she only claimed the credit."

"No way—she did it all by herself," Laurie said, defending me. "She marched straight into his dressing room and persuaded him to come. And that takes guts, which is more than you've got, Linda Holmann. Come on, Steph, we'll be late for class." She grabbed my arm and propelled me through the front doors. "Don't worry about them. It will take awhile for people to get used to it—then they'll all think you were really smart." Suddenly she stopped short, tugging on my arm. "Don't look now, but I think we've got a reception committee," she whispered to me. "And they don't look friendly."

Down the hall, waiting for us, O.P. was standing with Melissa. Patricia and some of her other friends were standing with them. Six pairs of accusing eyes stared at us as we walked toward them.

170

"Well, look who's here," Melissa drawled. "And who are you pretending to be today?" The girls behind her started to giggle.

"Last time I saw you you were awfully happy to know me," I said coldly. "You grabbed my arm and begged me to introduce you to Billy Case, if I remember correctly."

"Last time I thought you were somebody," Melissa snapped.

"Which just shows the sort of snobby person you are," I said. "I'm still the same person, only now I don't have the famous name to go with it. You and your crowd are all the same, you don't care about anyone at all. You only want to know important and famous people because you want some of their fame to rub off on you. Well, let me tell you something, Melissa—you have to earn importance. It's not something that rubs off. And it's not something you can steal from someone else, either," I said, turning to O.P.

"Thanks a lot, Stormy," he said coldly. "You realize that what you did last night wrecked my only chance to make the big time! Billy Case was so wrapped up in you and what you did that he didn't even remember how my group played. Boy, you really are dumb. To go to all that trouble for a little wimp like Charles—"

"He is not a wimp," I said, "and he's a million times more likely to make the big time than you, Oliver Pfeffelfinger, because he has one little thing that you lack—he has talent. Now if you'll excuse me, I'd like to go and find some real people to talk to." And I pushed past them, striding up the stairs without looking back.

"Boy, Steph, you really told them," Laurie said, panting as she ran to catch up with me.

"Yeah, I did, didn't I?" I said, looking back down the stairs and grinning. "I don't think they liked it very much, and I've probably made some enemies for life, but I don't really care. It felt good to stop pretending. In fact, it feels really good to be me again. Now if only I could talk to—"

"Look, there he is, going down the other staircase," Laurie cut me off suddenly.

I didn't stop to think. I dropped my schoolbag on the floor beside her and rushed after him. My feet clattered down those echoing halls. People turned to stare as I ran past them.

I caught up with him on the bottom step.

"Charles, please let's talk," I said. "I just want to explain—"

"There's nothing to explain," he said in a flat voice, looking down at the floor, his eyes not even meeting mine. "You're free to be whoever you want to be. You don't need my permission. Now, if you'll excuse me, I have a test starting in two minutes."

He went through the nearest door. I watched him go. *It's no use,* I thought, *I've lost him forever.*

172

Chapter Twenty-One

"Hey, cheer up, it's not the end of the world," Laurie said as we walked home.

"It feels like it," I said. "There's no way I can get Charles to listen to me. I suppose I'd better admit that he doesn't want me around anymore."

"I think he really does, Steph, but he's scared to be hurt again," Laurie said. "After all, you fooled him so completely once. But I know he likes you. After we all thought you had left the school, all he could do was talk about you."

"Really?"

"Yeah, nonstop—Stephanie this and Stephanie that. I think he's really crazy about you, underneath the hurt."

"You really think so?" I asked.

"I know so. And I think you should get him trapped in a corner and make him listen. If you have to, you might try tickling him mercilessly until he agrees he loves you."

"You're crazy," I said, but I giggled. I felt slightly hopeful again.

"No, I'm serious," she said. "Being Stormy was very good for you. It's given you loads of confidence. Look how you put down Melissa and O.P. this morning. You're a pretty tough person now. I bet you could win him back."

"He might not want a pretty tough person," I said.

"Oh, quit talking and go and try," she said. "And you'd better hurry, or his brother will be home from football practice. You don't want him listening in, do you?"

"OK," I said, "I'll go. But just this once. If he won't see me now, then I'll know it's the end."

"So what are you waiting for?" Laurie said, giving me a push. "Go get him, girl."

I turned back and smiled. "Thanks, Laurie, you're a real friend," I said.

It was a wild, wintery afternoon. Not really the sort of weather to be outdoors. More like an afternoon to curl up beside a fire. There was snow on the ground, and a bitter north wind danced through the trees, making more snow fall from the bare branches. The wind stung my face and took my breath away, but I didn't mind. Nothing could stop my determination. This was a day for setting things straight. I would talk to Charles, and I would make him listen.

I stomped up to his front door and hammered on it. The house was quiet, but his car was parked in the driveway. I hammered again. At last the sound of footsteps came from the inside.

"Who is it?" Charles's voice called through the door.

"It's Stephanie."

"Who?"

"Stephanie—you remember me, don't you? I've got to talk to you."

"I don't want to talk. Go away."

"I'm not going," I said loudly, "until you let me say what I want to say. Then if you never want to see me again, I'll go away, I promise. But I'm going to sit here on your doorstep until you open the door and listen to me. I don't care how long it takes, I'm not moving. And when they find my frozen body in the morning, they'll blame you."

"I'm not opening the door!" he yelled.

"OK, but I'm still not moving," I answered. I sank down onto the cold step.

The door opened a crack. "You're crazy," Charles said. "You'll catch pneumonia sitting there."

"So?" I said evenly. "It doesn't matter to you what I catch. You won't even let me talk to you."

Charles gave a big sigh. "Oh, OK. I suppose you'd better come inside," he said, opening the door wide. I followed him into the living room, that same family room where I had once danced with O.P.—it felt like a million years ago. Charles motioned toward a chair.

"Sit down," he said.

I sat.

"You really are Stephanie?" he asked.

I nodded. He shook his head in disbelief. "You

175

actually had me fooled," he said. "And everyone else, too. Why did you do it?"

"I didn't like the way I was before, I guess," I said. "You remember those tryouts and how they never really gave us a chance? I wanted to be the sort of person who did get a chance."

"And it worked, too," he said. "You were the star singer at the dance, you got Billy Case to come here, and you got Mr. Macho for a boyfriend."

"But I didn't get what I wanted," I said.

"What was that?"

"Real friends, I guess. People I could talk to, who cared about me. When I was Stormy, everyone wanted to know me just because they thought I was somebody. O.P. only took me out because he thought I could help him meet agents and get to the top. Now that they know I'm only Stephanie, they don't want to talk to me again."

"So why did you have to tell them? You could have kept quiet, and they'd never have known."

"Because of you, Charles," I said softly. "Because I didn't want to let you down. You see, I did keep my promise, or try to keep it. I was singing your song to myself at a rehearsal, and O.P. heard it. I didn't mean for anyone to overhear. I felt so bad when I knew he was trying to steal it. That's why I broke out of that supply closet and told everyone the truth."

There was a pause. I could hear the fire sputtering in the fireplace and the tick of a grandfather clock, also my own heart beating as if I'd just run a race.

"Why would you go to all that trouble, just for me?" Charles said at last.

"Because I care about you, I suppose," I said. "I didn't realize it before, or I'd never have gone through with this whole Stormy business. But I realized it when it hurt me to see you hurt and made me feel jealous when you were with someone else."

"You could have told me it was really you," he said.

"I wanted to. But if I had, you wouldn't have listened. You never gave me a chance," I said.

There was a pause. "You're right," he said. "I never did give you a chance. I thought Stephanie had walked out without telling me, and I didn't want to talk to her sister because she reminded me so much—I'm much too sensitive, I suppose. That's what my family always says, and I guess they're right."

We sat there in silence, each of us not knowing how to take the next step.

"You know what I think?" he said at last.

"What?"

"I think we've both been kind of dumb."

"I think you're right," I agreed. "But I've been much dumber than you have."

"No, I've been the dumb one."

"Hey, let's not start fighting about who's dumbest," I said, starting to laugh.

Charles started to laugh, too. He shook his head. "Now, if we could just get rid of that terrible haircut."

"That will have to grow out by itself," I said.

"And besides, what if I like it? You don't own me, you know."

His eyes were shining into mine. "I know. But I find it hard to kiss a girl when she looks like somebody else."

"Just close your eyes," I whispered. "Then you won't even notice."

"Good idea," he said. He put his hands on my shoulders and pulled me toward him. Then very gently his lips met mine. I remember thinking that if Charles was really as shy as I thought he was, how come he knew how to kiss so well? Then, as he wrapped his arms more firmly around me and his lips melted into mine, all my thoughts vanished except one—this was the kiss I had always dreamed about!

Chapter Twenty-Two

"You know, I'm glad every day's not like yesterday," I said to Charles. "I don't think I could stand the pace."

Charles laughed and put an arm around me. We were walking to school together, me dressed in ordinary clothes and without all the makeup. I looked up at Charles, and he bent to kiss my forehead. How could I ever have thought he was ordinary? Why hadn't I noticed how his eyes crinkled so nicely at the sides and the cute way his hair curled around his ears and that adorable little smile at the corners of his mouth.

"It's a big relief to be back to being me," I said. "You can't imagine what a strain it was to remember I was Stormy all the time."

"I wish that hair would hurry up and grow out," Charles said, tweaking a short curl. "Do you think we could buy you a wig?"

"No, we could not!" I said. "Actually I kind of like my hair. Well, the blond part, anyway. I think I'll stay blond. After all, they do have more fun!"

"I thought you looked just fine before," Charles said. "But I have to admit that blond hair makes your eyes look fantastic."

And so we went up the steps into school. As we walked down the halls together, people stopped and stared at the sight of former rock singer Stormy Fenton, now without any of her disguise, walking hand in hand with former nobody, now identified as great song writer, Charles Patterson. And I didn't mind their stares one bit. I stared right back at them with a sort of self-satisfied grin on my face that said, "Don't you wish you were me? I'm much luckier than you."

And not for a moment did I regret the passing of Stormy. I remembered how sweet it had been when everyone had cheered after I sang and how people crowded around me all the time. But I knew, absolutely and definitely, that I would rather be me and have Charles and real friends than have all the glory I got from being Stormy.

I didn't get a chance to see Laurie until we were in Mrs. Carr's geometry class together. Mrs. Carr was a strict teacher who did not allow whispering, and so I wrote Laurie a note and tossed it onto her desk.

"It worked. I saw him. Everything is Great," I wrote.

Almost immediately a note came zooming back to me. "Can I be a bridesmaid? I look terrific in pale blue," Laurie had written.

I started to giggle.

"If you find my class so amusing that you have to laugh, I suggest you wait outside the door until the other students have left, Stephanie Fenton," Mrs. Carr said in her grating voice. "You may do your assignment after school."

"Nothing's amusing, Mrs. Carr," I said, frowning down at my book. I was not going to miss a single moment of being with Charles by staying after school. I didn't dare look at Laurie again all period.

I thought that all the good things in the world had already happened that day, but I was wrong. Grandma and I were just sitting down to dinner when Charles arrived on the front doorstep. He was panting and looked very excited. It seemed that Billy Case's manager had paid him a visit and wanted to record his song.

"I thought it was so private and personal you didn't want anyone to hear it," I said, teasing him.

Charles blushed. "Only because I thought they might laugh or think it was no good," he said. "But when I heard that a big star actually wanted to record it—why, I could put myself through college with that kind of money."

"And take your girlfriend out for pizza," I said, winding my arms around his neck. "I'm very proud of you," I whispered. "But you should have listened to me in the first place when I told you the song was good. I have very good taste, particularly in boys!"

Charles sat down and ate dinner with us—alfalfa sprouts and all. We had just finished and were about to go out when the telephone rang. I ran to answer it. "Fenton residence," I said.

"Is that you, Stephanie?" came a distant voice on the other end.

"Daddy? What's wrong?"

"Why, nothing's wrong, honey. I just wanted to talk to my little girl. How are you, Stephanie? We've been thinking about you so much. Your mother has been worrying that you're not eating properly or that you're mixing with all the wrong people."

"Daddy, I'm fine. I couldn't be better. Everything is going so well, and I have lots of friends and one particular friend who is terrific." I let my eyes wander across to Charles, and he winked at me.

"What sort of friend?" my father questioned.

"Oh, about five-ten, brown hair, nice eyes, and a smile like Christopher Reeve."

"You mean a boy?" My father sounded surprised. "You have a boyfriend?"

"Well, I don't know too many girls who smile like Christopher Reeve," I said calmly. "He's very nice, Daddy. He's the sort of boy even you would approve of."

"Well, that's nice, honey," he said hesitantly. "I'll look forward to meeting him."

"Oh, I wish you could, Dad, then you could see how great everything is and tell Mom to stop worrying."

"Your wish can be granted, honey," he said. "I plan to be there tomorrow morning."

"Tomorrow?" I barely choked out. "All the way from Saudi Arabia?"

He laughed. "No, all the way from New York City. I'm in town for a three-day conference, but I got here a day early so that I could see my little girl."

I felt a moment's panic. It was all very easy speaking to a father you knew was half a world away, but when he was going to show up in a few hours. . . . "That's terrific, Dad," I said. "Is Mom with you?"

"Unfortunately not. They wouldn't pay her fare back for just three days. I can tell you, Steph, she's not liking it too much over there, and I can't say I am, either."

"What's wrong with it, Dad?"

"Too many darn rules, that's what's wrong. Everything's so strict. Women aren't allowed to drive cars; they aren't allowed to wear jeans—you aren't allowed to do this, and you aren't allowed to do that. It's like being in a jail, I tell you."

I started to smile. By the time I hung up, I was grinning from ear to ear.

"You look very pleased with yourself," Charles commented. "That was your father, I gather."

"He's in New York, Charles."

"Back in New York? They're not going to take you home, are they?" He looked worried. I smiled.

"Relax. He's only here for a couple of days on business, but he's coming to visit me tomorrow. You can meet him after school if you're on your best behavior."

"Yes, ma'am," he said happily. "So you were only smiling because you'll be glad to see him again?"

"That, too," I said. "But mostly I'm smiling because I think my parents are beginning to see how it feels to live with too many rules."

"You think they'll give you more freedom when they come back?"

"I'm sure of it. When they see how wisely I've chosen my friends and—"

"Your hair," Charles said suddenly. "What will your father say when he sees your hair?"

My hand flew up to my short curls, and I glanced at myself in the living room mirror. Then I grinned at him. "He's just going to have to put up with it," I said. "I'll tell him that it's my hair and this is the way I choose to wear it right now."

"Well, good for you," Charles said. "You've come a long way."

"Yes, I have," I said as I reached my hand out to him. Together we went out into the clear, frosty night.

You'll fall in love with all the Sweet Dream romances. Reading these stories, you'll be reminded of yourself or of someone you know. There's Jennie, the *California Girl*, who becomes an outsider when her family moves to Texas. And Cindy, the *Little Sister*, who's afraid that Christine, the oldest in the family, will steal her new boyfriend. Don't miss any of the Sweet Dreams romances.

☐ 24327	**SECRET IDENTITY #22** Joanna Campbell	$2.25
☐ 24407	**FALLING IN LOVE AGAIN #23** Barbara Conklin	$2.25
☐ 24329	**THE TROUBLE WITH CHARLIE #24** Jaye Ellen	$2.25
☐ 22543	**HER SECRET SELF #25** Rhondi Villot	$1.95
☐ 24292	**IT MUST BE MAGIC #26** Marian Woodruff	$2.25
☐ 22681	**TOO YOUNG FOR LOVE #27** Gailanne Maravel	$1.95
☐ 23053	**TRUSTING HEARTS #28** Jocelyn Saal	$1.95
☐ 24312	**NEVER LOVE A COWBOY #29** Jesse Dukore	$2.25
☐ 24293	**LITTLE WHITE LIES #30** Lois I. Fisher	$2.25
☐ 23189	**TOO CLOSE FOR COMFORT #31** Debra Spector	$1.95
☐ 24837	**DAYDREAMER #32** Janet Quin-Harkin	$2.25
☐ 23283	**DEAR AMANDA #33** Rosemary Vernon	$1.95
☐ 23287	**COUNTRY GIRL #34** Melinda Pollowitz	$1.95
☐ 24336	**FORBIDDEN LOVE #35** Marian Woodruff	$2.25
☐ 24338	**SUMMER DREAMS #36** Barbara Conklin	$2.25
☐ 23340	**PORTRAIT OF LOVE #37** Jeanette Noble	$1.95
☐ 24331	**RUNNING MATES #38** Jocelyn Saal	$2.25
☐ 24340	**FIRST LOVE #39** Debra Spector	$2.25
☐ 24315	**SECRETS #40** Anna Aaron	$2.25
☐ 24838	**THE TRUTH ABOUT ME AND BOBBY V. #41** Janetta Johns	$2.25
☐ 23532	**THE PERFECT MATCH #42** Marian Woodruff	$1.95

Prices and availability subject to change without notice.

Bantam Books, Inc., Dept. SD, 414 East Golf Road, Des Plaines, Ill. 60016

Please send me the books I have checked above. I am enclosing $_____
(please add $1.25 to cover postage and handling). Send check or money order
—no cash or C.O.D.'s please.

Mr/Mrs/Miss_____

Address_____

City_____ State/Zip_____

SD—11/84

Please allow four to six weeks for delivery. This offer expires 5/85.